LEVEL E

STECK-VAUGHN

MW00973487

FOCUS ON
SCIENCE™

PROGRAM CONSULTANT
Elizabeth Maryott
Instructor, Mathematics-Science Division
Wayne State College
Wayne, Nebraska

REVIEWER
Joan Ford, Nationally Board Certified Teacher
Hudson Local School District
Hudson, Ohio

STECK-VAUGHN
ELEMENTARY · SECONDARY · ADULT · LIBRARY
A Harcourt Company

Acknowledgments

STAFF CREDITS

Executive Editor: Diane Sharpe

Project Team Leaders: Jim Cauthron, Design; Janet Jerzycki, Editorial

Editor: Linda Bullock

Design Manager: Jim Cauthron

Cover Design: Jim Cauthron

Cover Electronic Production: Alan Klemp

Program Development, Design, Illustration, and Production:
Proof Positive/Farrowlyne Associates, Inc.

PHOTOGRAPHY AND ILLUSTRATION CREDITS

Cover and Title page © D. Lehman/Westlight; p. 5 John Neubauer/PhotoEdit; p. 6 Ken Lucas/Visuals Unlimited; p. 7 Background photo © PhotoDisk; p. 8 Corel Photo Studio; p.10 Corel Photo Studio; p.12 Joel Snyder; p. 14a Paul Fuqua; p. 14b Corel Photo Studio; p.16 Corel Photo Studio; p. 18 Tek-Nēk, Inc.; p. 20 Kathie Kelleher; p. 22 Ken Lucas/Visuals Unlimited; p. 23 Background photo © PhotoDisk; p. 24 Tek-Nēk, Inc.; p. 26 Tek-Nēk, Inc.; p. 27 Tek-Nēk, Inc.; p. 28a & b Tek-Nēk, Inc.; p. 30 Joel Snyder; p. 32a Tek-Nēk, Inc.; p. 32b John D. Cunningham/Visuals Unlimited; p. 34a & b Corel Photo Studio; p. 36 Joel Snyder; p. 38 Andrew Syred/Tony Stone Images; p. 39 Background photo © PhotoDisk; p. 40 Tek-Nēk, Inc.; p. 42 Tek-Nēk, Inc.; p. 44a & b Tek-Nēk, Inc.; p. 46a & b Tek-Nēk, Inc.; p. 47 Sandy McMahon; p. 48 Tek-Nēk, Inc.; p. 50a & b Tek-Nēk, Inc.; p. 52 Kathie Kelleher; p. 54a E. Weber/Visuals Unlimited; 54b Alice Prescott/Unicorn Stock Photos; p. 54c David Young-Wolff/PhotoEdit; p. 55 Doug Sokell/Visuals Unlimited; p. 56 Art Wolfe/Tony Stone Images; p. 57 Background photo © PhotoDisk; p. 58 Tek-Nēk, Inc.; p. 60 Corel Photo Studio; p. 62a & b Corel Photo Studio; p. 64 Corel Photo Studio; p. 66 Corel Photo Studio; p. 68 Tek-Nēk, Inc.; p. 70 Kathie Kelleher; p.72 Brian Stablyk/Tony Stone Images; p. 73 Background photo © PhotoDisk; p. 74a PP/FA, Inc.; p. 74b Ulrike Welsch/PhotoEdit; p. 76 Tek-Nēk, Inc.; p. 78 Corel Photo Studio; p. 80 Corel Photo Studio; p. 82 Tek-Nēk, Inc.; p. 84a Tek-Nēk, Inc.; p. 84b Corel Photo Studio; p. 86 Kathie Kelleher; p. 88 Timothy Marshall/Tony Stone Images; p. 89 Background photo © PhotoDisk; p. 90 Joel Snyder; p. 92 Tek-Nēk, Inc.; p. 94a Chris Windle; p. 94b Tek-Nēk, Inc.; p. 96a & b Tek-Nēk, Inc.; p. 98a & b Leslie Dunlap; p. 100 Tek-Nēk, Inc.; p. 102 Joel Snyder; p. 104a Corel Photo Studio; p. 104b Corel Photo Studio; 104c LINK/Visuals Unlimited; p. 105 Orion Press/Tony Stone Images; p. 106 RNHRD NHS Trust/Tony Stone Images; p. 107 Background photo © PhotoDisk; p. 108a & b Tek-Nēk, Inc.; p. 110a Tek-Nēk, Inc.; p. 110b Joel Snyder; p. 110c Tek-Nēk, Inc.; p. 111a,b,c Tek-Nēk, Inc.; p. 112 Joel Snyder; p. 114 Chris Windle; p. 116 Mary Kate Denny/PhotoEdit; p. 118 Chris Windle; p. 120 Kathie Kelleher; p. 122 Dennis MacDonald/PhotoEdit; p. 123 Background photo © PhotoDisk; p. 124a Joel Snyder; p. 124b Corel Photo Studio; p. 126 Joel Snyder; p. 128a,b,c Leslie Dunlap; p. 130 Corel Photo Studio; p. 132a & b Joel Snyder; p. 134a ramp Michael Newman/PhotoEdit; p. 134b Corel Photo Studio; p. 134c LINK/Visuals Unlimited; p. 136 Kathie Kelleher; p.138a © Lonnie Duka/Tony Stone Images; p. 138b Tony Freeman/Photo Edit; p.138c © Kevin Horan/Tony Stone Images

ISBN: 0-8172-8031-6

Copyright © 1999 Steck-Vaughn Company
All rights reserved. No part of the material protected by this copyright may be reproduced in any form by any means, electronic or mechanical, including photocopying, recording, or by any information storage and retrieval system, without permission in writing from the copyright owner. Requests for permission to make copies of any part of the work should be mailed to: Copyright Permissions, Steck-Vaughn Company, P.O. Box 26015, Austin, Texas 78755. Printed in the United States of America.

9 0 DBH 04 03

Contents

Unit 1

Life Science

There has been life on Earth for millions of years. Some living things are *extinct*—they no longer exist. To show what ancient living things looked like, many museums display fossils, which are traces of living things preserved in rocks. This photograph presents a display of dinosaur bones. Some dinosaurs were small, but others were larger than any land animal on Earth today.

Plants Over Time

Plants didn't always look the way they do today. The first plants were tiny and lived in seawater. Over time, plants moved onto land. Beautifully preserved in rock, this fossil of an ancient fern hints at what land plants looked like millions of years ago. It may be that when this plant was alive, there were no trees anywhere on Earth. In this chapter you will learn about the history of plants.

What is it?

- It is more than 400 million years old.
- Its tissues carry water, nutrients, and food.
- Early ones looked like stems lying on the ground.

LESSON 1

What Were the First Plants?

What do you think of when you hear the word *plants*? You probably think of bushes, flowers, and trees. But the first plants on Earth were very different from most plants you see today.

Scientists who study ancient plants are called paleobotanists. Paleobotanists learn about these plants by studying **fossils**. Fossils are traces of early life that have been preserved in rocks. Paleobotanists don't know exactly when the first plants appeared. But some fossils suggest a simple kind of tiny plant may have appeared over two billion years ago.

What did these plants look like? Paleobotanists can't know that for sure, either. But they are certain that the first plants lived only in the water. These early water plants were tiny, simple plants that floated in the ocean, drifting with the currents.

Like the plants of today, the first plants used sunlight to make food. This process is called **photosynthesis**. So the first plants had to live on or close to the surface of the water, where they could get enough sunlight.

The first plants formed from even smaller living things that used photosynthesis. You might have seen green algae, which is sometimes called "pond scum." It's likely that green algae is like the ancestors of early plants. It is interesting to look at green algae and imagine looking at some of the earliest living things on Earth—things that were living more than two billion years ago!

The plants of so long ago are now **extinct**, which means they are no longer alive. But in a way, they live on because they are the ancestors of all the plants you see today.

The algae on the surface of this pond may look like the ancestors of early plants.

A. Write the word that best completes each sentence.

billion   paleobotanists   water

extinct   photosynthesis

1. Scientists who study ancient plants are called

   _____.

2. The first plants appeared on Earth about two _____ years ago.

3. The first plants lived only in the _____.

4. Like plants today, the first plants made their food through a process called

   _____.

5. The first plants are no longer alive, which means they are

   _____.

B. Put a ✔ next to each sentence that correctly describes the first plants.

_____ 1. The first plants looked like most plants we see today.

_____ 2. Many fossils of the first plants have been found.

_____ 3. The first plants were tiny.

_____ 4. The first plants lived on or close to the surface of the water.

_____ 5. Ancestors of the first plants may have looked something like green algae.

C. Write one or more sentences to answer the question.

Why do you think scientists have been unable to find fossils of the first plants?

_____

_____

_____

_____

LESSON 2

What Were the First Land Plants?

You have learned that more than a billion years ago, the very first plants on Earth lived only in the water. Millions of years later, the first land plants appeared. Since then, land plants have continued to change. The first water plants were the ancestors of the land plants we know today, such as the oak tree and the rosebush.

When did the first land plants appear? No one knows for sure. But paleobotanists think land plants first appeared about 430 million years ago.

Where did the first land plants grow? Do you remember where their ancestors lived? The first land plants grew along the shores of oceans and lakes. Many areas of the shore are covered by water much of the time. Even when shores are not under water, they are muddy places. The water keeps the soil damp. This condition probably made the change from water to land easier. The damp, muddy shores of Earth were the homes for the first land plants.

What did the first land plants look like? They probably looked a lot like their ancestors, the water plants. The water plants depended on water to help support their weight. They did not need stems to hold them up. The first land plants did not have stems to support their weight either. They did not have roots or leaves. They simply lay on top of the mud. The bottoms of these plants soaked up water from the damp soil. The tops of these plants captured light from the sun for photosynthesis.

Although they were small and simple, the first land plants were important pioneers. They made the great change from life in the water to life on land. These first land plants became the ancestors of all the land plants that followed.

The first land plants grew along muddy shores.

A.

Write <u>water plants</u> or <u>land plants</u> or <u>both</u> to answer each question.

1. Which came first, land plants or water plants?

   _____

2. Which first appeared over a billion years ago?

   _____

3. Which first appeared about 430 million years ago?

   _____

4. Which used sunlight to make food? _____

B.

Write the missing word or words in each sentence.

1. The first water plants were the _____ of land plants.

   (fossils, ancestors, seeds)

2. The damp, muddy _____ of Earth were the homes
   of the first land plants.

   (algae, shores, oceans)

3. The first land plants were important _____ because
   they made the change from life in the water to life on land.

   (pioneers, fossils, oak trees)

C.

Put a ✔ next to each sentence that correctly describes the first land plants.

_____ 1. The first land plants developed from earlier water plants.

_____ 2. The first land plants grew along the shore.

_____ 3. The first land plants may have grown on top of mud.

_____ 4. The first land plants had stems, roots, and leaves.

_____ 5. The first land plants used photosynthesis.

D.

Write one or more sentences to answer the questions.

Would the first land plants have been able to live on top of a rock sticking out of
the water? Why or why not?

_____

_____

3 What Are Vascular Plants?

You have learned that the first land plants were like their ancestors, the water plants. Millions of years passed before land plants began to look like the plants you see today. This change began with the appearance of **vascular plants**, more than 400 million years ago.

Vascular plants are plants that have special tissues called **xylem** and **phloem**. Xylem tissues carry water and nutrients through the plant. Phloem tissues carry food made by plants during photosynthesis. Today, most of the world's plants are vascular plants.

Early vascular plants looked like green stems stretching across the ground. Some of these stems branched. Some of the branches grew upward, toward the sun. The first vascular plants had only stems. It took time for leaves and roots to appear.

Over millions of years, vascular plants spread across the land. They began to grow in climates different from the climates of their ancestors. Changes began to appear. For example, plants that spread to dry areas, such as deserts, developed roots to hold them in the soil and take in water. Plants that lived in shady places developed leaves with special shapes to capture more sunlight. These changes in vascular plants took millions of years to happen.

Soon after vascular plants began to appear, two important kinds of vascular plants developed. They were **ferns** and **conifers**. Ferns appeared first, about 400 million years ago. They are leafy, green plants that grow in shady, damp places. Conifers appeared about 300 million years ago. They are trees and shrubs that hold their seeds in cones. Pine trees and fir trees are both conifers. When you look at a fern or a conifer, you are seeing what many plants looked like hundreds of millions of years ago!

This picture shows what early vascular plants may have looked like.

A.

Draw a line from each word to the words that describe it.

1. vascular   plants that hold their seeds in cones

2. xylem   tissues that carry food made during photosynthesis through the plant

3. phloem   tissues that carry water and nutrients through the plant

4. ferns   plants that have special tissues to carry water and food

5. conifers   leafy plants that grow in shady, damp areas

B.

Write one or more sentences to answer the questions.

1. What did the first vascular plants look like? Describe them.

_____

_____

2. What changes did vascular plants make?

_____

_____

C.

Put a ✔ next to each sentence that correctly describes vascular plants.

_____ 1. Vascular plants were the first land plants.

_____ 2. Vascular plants have special tissues that carry water and food through the plant.

_____ 3. There are very few vascular plants in the world today.

_____ 4. Vascular plants appeared more than 400 million years ago.

_____ 5. Vascular plants developed stems, roots, and leaves.

D.

Write one or more sentences to answer the question.

Most of the plants in the world are vascular plants. What does this tell you about how vascular tissues are helpful to plants?

_____

_____

4 What Are Flowering Plants?

You have learned that more than 400 million years ago, the first vascular plants appeared. Only 100 million years later, Earth was covered with green plants. Many of them would have looked familiar to you. But there still wasn't a single flower in the world!

Flowering plants, or plants that produce flowers, first appeared about 100 million years ago. Since then, they have been very successful. There are about 300,000 **species**, or kinds, of plants in the world. More than three fourths of them are flowering plants. Most of the plants you know, including most trees and bushes, and most of the plants people eat, are flowering plants.

It might surprise you to learn that many of the flowering plants you see today look like the first flowering plants on Earth. The first flowering plants looked much like buttercups, water lilies, magnolias, and sycamores.

Many flowering plants need insects to help them **reproduce**, or make new plants. The bright colors and sweet smells of flowers invite insects. The flowers make **nectar**, or food, for the insects. When insects land on a flower, pollen sticks to their bodies. **Pollen** is a yellow dust that flowering plants make to help them reproduce. As insects travel from flower to flower looking for food, they carry pollen with them. When they land on another plant, the pollen joins with the second plant. This allows the plant to make seeds. These steps are called **pollination**.

Pollination has proved to be a good way for plants to reproduce. There are more flowering plants than any other kind of plant on Earth. Flowering plants are Earth's youngest plants, but they continue to grow and spread.

Some of the first flowering plants looked much like a buttercup.

Bees help flowering plants reproduce by spreading pollen.

A. Write the missing word or words in each sentence.

1. Flowering plants first appeared about 100 _____ years ago.

   (thousand, million, billion)

2. Another word for species is _____.

   (kinds, plants, pollen)

3. Most plants on Earth are _____.

   (ferns, flowering plants, conifers)

4. Plants reproduce when they make _____.

   (more flowers, bright colors, new plants)

5. The yellow dust that flowering plants make is called

   _____.

   (pollen, flower, phloem)

B. Put a ✔ next to each sentence that correctly describes flowering plants.

_____ 1. Flowering plants are the oldest kinds of land plants.

_____ 2. The first flowering plants looked like many flowering plants today.

_____ 3. Most flowering plants need insects to help them reproduce.

C. Write one or more sentences to answer the question.

How are flowering plants and insects partners?

_____

_____

_____

_____

_____

How Have Plants and Animals Changed Together?

Plants have changed in many important ways since they first appeared on Earth. From tiny, simple plants, they have developed into thousands of species of plants of every shape, size, and color. They first lived only in water. Now they live in water and on land. These changes happened slowly, over hundreds of millions of years.

But plants were not the only living things that changed over this time. Animals changed, too. Plants and animals have changed together because plants and animals are the two great partners in life on Earth. From the earliest times, animals have needed plants to live. Plants provide animals with food. Even animals who eat other animals need plants. This is because the animals they eat need plants to live.

So when plants changed over time, the animals changed, too. For example, some early plants grew leaves filled with poison. Since animals would not eat the leaves, the plants lived and reproduced. The animals had to look for food from other kinds of plants. But over millions of years, some animals slowly changed so that they would not be hurt by the poison. The change in the plant led to a change in the animals that ate them.

Many of the changes plants have made help animals, too. You know that most flowering plants need insects to carry pollen to the same kinds of plants. The insects need food. They have more food if they don't have to share with many other insects. Some plants have changed so that only a few insects can reach the nectar. The plants feed only these insects, and the insects help the plants reproduce.

Animals need plants to live. As plants have changed, so have animals.

A.

Write <u>True</u> if the sentence is true. Write <u>False</u> if the sentence is false.

_____ 1. Both plants and animals have changed over hundreds of millions of years.

_____ 2. Even animals that don't eat plants need plants to live.

_____ 3. Some early plants grew leaves filled with poison.

_____ 4. When plants changed, animals also changed so that they could still eat the plants.

_____ 5. None of the changes in animals and plants helped either group.

_____ 6. Flowering plants do not need insects.

B.

Write the word or words that best complete each sentence.

animals	food	sometimes
each other	plants	

1. Plants and _____ have changed together.

2. The changes in _____ and animals took place over hundreds of millions of years.

3. Plants provide animals with _____.

4. Changes in plants have _____ hurt animals.

5. Plants and animals need _____ to live.

C.

Write one or more sentences to answer the question.

Imagine a plant starts to grow thorns. How might an animal change so it could still eat parts of the plant?

_____

_____

_____

_____

_____

How Do People Change Plants?

Not all of the changes in plants have happened because of nature. Many changes in plants have been made on purpose by people. The first people who changed plants lived about 10,000 years ago. These people were the first farmers. For thousands of years, people had eaten wild plants. The first farmers learned they could grow the plants themselves. That way, food would always be available nearby.

To begin farming, they gathered seeds from wild plants to grow on their land. Of course, they gathered seeds only from the plants that were the best to eat. And they chose seeds only from the healthiest plants. The plants that grew from these seeds became the first crops.

Year after year, the farmers kept planting only the seeds from their crops. That way, the new plants would always be the healthiest and the best ones to eat. Over time, these plants changed because they were separated from the wild plants. For example, wild corn grows small ears with just a few kernels, or seeds. Early farmers planted only the corn that grew the largest ears with the most kernels. By keeping these crops separate from the wild plants, over time all the crop corn grew large ears with many kernels. Crop plants that people have separated in this way from their wild ancestors are called **domesticated plants**.

Today, people still change plants. Sometimes two different species of plants are combined. For example, one kind of corn grows large ears. Another kind of corn grows very quickly. By joining these two species, people have created a kind of corn that both grows quickly and has large ears. Plants that are joined in this way are called **hybrid plants**.

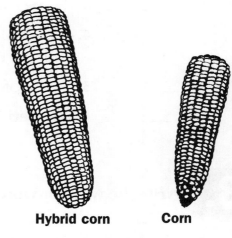

Hybrid corn   **Corn**

The hybrid corn has larger ears than regular corn.

A. Write the missing word or words in each sentence.

1. The first _____ lived about 10,000 years ago.

   (hunters, farmers, wild plants)

2. The first farmers used seeds from the _____ wild plants.

   (healthiest, smallest, first)

3. People _____ made some changes in plants.

   (accidentally, purposely, never)

4. The plants that people grew away from wild plants are called

   _____ plants.

   (separated, domesticated, hybrid)

5. New plants that are made by joining different kinds of plants are called

   _____ plants.

   (separated, domesticated, hybrid)

B. Write <u>True</u> if the sentence is true. Write <u>False</u> if the sentence is false.

_____ 1. People still change plants today.

_____ 2. People sometimes change plants to make better crops.

_____ 3. It is impossible for people to change plants.

C. Write one or more sentences to answer the question.

People sometimes change plants so that the plants produce more food. What is another reason people might have for changing plants?

_____

_____

_____

_____

_____

Observe Growing Plants

You need:

- **2 cups**
- **soil**
- **8 seeds**
- **water**
- **notebook**
- **ruler**

In this activity you will see how light affects growing plants.

Follow these steps:

1. Fill two cups with soil. Plant four seeds in each cup. Cover the seeds with soil.

2. Add just enough water to the cups to make the soil damp.

3. Place one cup in a light place and the other cup in a dark place. Add water every few days to keep the soil damp.

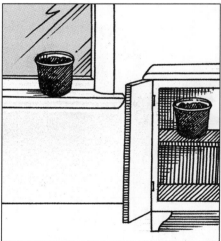

4. After two weeks, remove one plant from each cup. Measure the roots, stems, and leaves of both plants. Draw and label a diagram of each plant.

Write answers to these questions.

1. How did the plants change over two weeks?

_____

_____

_____

2. How does light affect plants?

_____

_____

Darken the circle next to the correct answer.

1. What do we call scientists who study ancient plants?
   - Ⓐ paleobotanists
   - Ⓑ farmers
   - Ⓒ planters
   - Ⓓ hybrids

2. What were the first plants on Earth?
   - Ⓐ hybrids
   - Ⓑ vascular plants
   - Ⓒ conifers
   - Ⓓ water plants

3. The first land plants developed from
   - Ⓐ vascular plants.
   - Ⓑ water plants.
   - Ⓒ flowering plants.
   - Ⓓ hybrid plants.

4. Where did the first land plants grow?
   - Ⓐ in the water
   - Ⓑ along the shore
   - Ⓒ in the mountains
   - Ⓓ in the desert

5. What do the special tissues in vascular plants carry?
   - Ⓐ pollen
   - Ⓑ xylem and phloem
   - Ⓒ photosynthesis
   - Ⓓ food and water

6. Ferns and conifers are examples of
   - Ⓐ the first plants on Earth.
   - Ⓑ early hybrid plants.
   - Ⓒ early vascular plants.
   - Ⓓ early water plants.

7. Another word for *kinds* of plants is
   - Ⓐ species.
   - Ⓑ hybrids.
   - Ⓒ fossils.
   - Ⓓ ferns.

8. Flowering plants reproduce by
   - Ⓐ vascular tissues.
   - Ⓑ pollination.
   - Ⓒ photosynthesis.
   - Ⓓ roots, leaves, and stems.

9. Which of the following statements is correct?
   - Ⓐ No animals need plants to live.
   - Ⓑ Some animals need plants to live.
   - Ⓒ All animals need plants to live.
   - Ⓓ Only animals that lived long ago needed plants.

10. Wild plants that have been turned into crops are called
    - Ⓐ domesticated plants.
    - Ⓑ hybrid plants.
    - Ⓒ vascular plants.
    - Ⓓ land plants.

Animals Over Time

Look carefully at the animal in this picture. What you are seeing is the hard outer skeleton of an extinct animal called a trilobite. Look at the head and find the animal's eyes. Look at the back and find the three sections there. The name *trilobite* comes from those three sections. Although trilobites looked like insects, they lived in the sea. Their closest living relatives are crabs. In this chapter you will learn about the history of animals.

What is it?

- It is a vertebrate.
- It can live its entire life on land.
- It first appeared about 280 million years ago.

What Were the First Animals?

Earth is the only place where we know there is life. Special microscopes let scientists see examples of the oldest known life on Earth. They are fossils found in rocks that are about 3.5 billion years old. These first living things were bacteria. Billions of years passed before the first plants appeared. Then, hundreds of millions more years passed before animal life appeared.

Like the life before it, the first animal life appeared in Earth's oceans. Ancestors of the first animals were simple, one-celled creatures. One-celled means their entire body is made of just one cell. They were so small that their fossils can be seen only with a microscope.

Soft-bodied animals and hard-bodied animals lived in the ocean millions of years ago.

The first animal life appeared about 600 million years ago. The first animals were many-celled. Many-celled means their bodies are made of more than one cell. At first, all of the cells were the same. But over a long time, groups of cells began to do different jobs, such as digesting food and reproducing.

The first many-celled animals were **soft-bodied** animals, or animals without bones or shells. Millions of years ago, Earth's oceans held many different kinds of soft-bodied animals. Many were like jellyfish or worms. Others were strange creatures unlike anything alive today.

Over time, some soft-bodied animals grew larger. They developed hard coverings and bones to support their growth. These **hard-bodied** animals included mollusks, such as clams, starfish, and trilobites. Trilobites were animals that usually crawled on the bottom of the ocean. In their time, they were very successful animals. Fossils show that trilobites lived in Earth's oceans for more than 300 million years before becoming extinct.

A.

Write True if the sentence is true. Write False if the sentence is false.

_____ 1. The first animal life appeared on Earth before the first plants.

_____ 2. Many-celled animals developed into one-celled animals.

_____ 3. Hard-bodied animals were one-celled.

B.

Write the missing word in each sentence.

1. Fossils of _____ are examples of the oldest known life on Earth.

   (trilobites, bacteria, mollusks)

2. The first animals were _____ creatures.

   (one-celled, many-celled, hard-bodied)

3. Jellyfish and worms are two examples of _____ animals.

   (one-celled, soft-bodied, hard-bodied)

C.

Draw a line from each word to the words that describe it.

1. one-celled   animals with bones or shells

2. many-celled   animals without bones or shells

3. soft-bodied   early animals that crawled on the bottom of the ocean

4. hard-bodied   made up of more than one cell

5. trilobites   made up of just one cell

D.

Write one or more sentences to answer the question.

Hard body coverings and bones help support the bodies of animals. How might hard body coverings help animals live longer?

_____

_____

2 What Are Fish?

The first animals on Earth lived in the ocean, but they were not fish. The first animals were **invertebrates,** or animals without backbones. The first **vertebrates,** or animals with backbones, were fish. A fish is a vertebrate animal that lives in water.

The first fish appeared about 480 million years ago. These early fish are called ostracoderms. Ostracoderms had a strong, bony covering, or armor. This heavy armor probably made swimming difficult. Ostracoderms were **jawless fish,** which means they had no jaws. They sucked food from the ocean floor. Today, the only jawless fish are lampreys and hagfish. Like their ancestors, these fish must suck their food.

Over millions of years, some jawless fish developed jaws. We call them **jawed fish.** Jawed fish can bite and hold food in their mouths. They first appeared about 400 million years ago. Today, almost all of the fish in the world are jawed fish.

There are two main groups of jawed fish. One group has skeletons that are made mostly of **cartilage.** Cartilage is a tough tissue, like the hard tissue in your outer ear. The earliest jawed fish had skeletons made of cartilage. Today, sharks, skates, and rays have skeletons made of cartilage. The other group of jawed fish are called **bony fish.** Bony fish are fish with skeletons made mostly of bone. Most fishes in the world today are bony fish. Bony fish first appeared about 380 million years ago.

The first modern fish appeared about 190 million years ago. These fish are better swimmers than their ancestors. Today there are nearly 25,000 species of fish of all shapes, sizes, and colors. They live in almost all of Earth's water. For these reasons, fish are one of the most successful kinds of animal life on Earth.

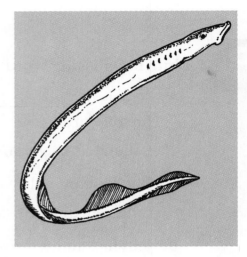

Today's jawless lamprey has a cartilage skeleton like the first fish that appeared about 480 million years ago.

Bony fish first appeared about 380 million years ago.

A. The sentences below tell how fish developed. Write 1, 2, 3, and 4 to show the correct order.

_____ Bony fish developed.

_____ The first modern fish developed.

_____ Jawed fish developed.

_____ The first fish developed.

B. Write the word or words that best complete each sentence.

bony fish	**invertebrates**	**jawless fish**	**vertebrates**
cartilage	**jawed fish**	**ostracoderms**	

1. Animals without backbones are called _____.

2. Animals with backbones are called _____.

3. The first fish, which appeared about 480 million years ago, were called

_____.

4. Ostracoderms were _____, which means they had no jaws.

5. Fish that can bite and hold food in their mouths are called

_____.

6. The earliest fish had skeletons made of _____.

7. Fish with skeletons made mostly of bone are called

_____.

C. Write one or more sentences to answer the question.

What advantages would a jawed fish have over a jawless fish?

_____

_____

_____

What Are Insects and Amphibians?

Until about 500 million years ago, all animal life on Earth lived in the oceans. There were no land animals. Then, animals that could live on land developed from some water animals. One of the first kinds of animals to make the change from life in the water to life on land was **insects**. Insects are tiny, invertebrate animals with six legs. Beetles, flies, bees, and ants are common insects.

Insects are the most common animals on Earth.

Insects first appeared on land at least 400 million years ago. Today, scientists describe insects as the most successful of all animals. Eight out of every ten species of animals on Earth are insects. There may be as many as ten million different species of insects. If all the world's insects were spread evenly across Earth, there would be more than two billion insects living in every square mile. Insects have many shapes, colors, and sizes. They live in every environment, from deserts to mountains to forests.

The first vertebrates to come from the water to live on land were **amphibians**. Amphibians are animals that live part of their lives in water and part on land. Common amphibians today include frogs, toads, and salamanders.

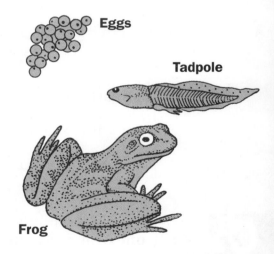

Amphibians live part of their lives in water and part on land.

The first amphibians appeared about 360 million years ago. They developed, over millions of years, from kinds of fish that had lungs and strong fins. At first, these fish could survive out of the water only for short periods of time. Perhaps they used their strong fins to drag themselves across the mud from one pool of water to the next. Slowly, their bodies changed so they could live on land. Their fins developed into legs. On land, they found food among the plants and insects. But they lived only in wet, swampy areas near water. They returned to the water to lay their eggs.

A.

Write _True_ if the sentence is true. Write _False_ if the sentence is false.

_____ 1. Insects are tiny animals with six legs.

_____ 2. Amphibians are the most successful kinds of animals.

_____ 3. Insects developed about 400 million years ago.

_____ 4. Amphibians were the first vertebrates to live on land.

_____ 5. One example of an amphibian is a toad.

_____ 6. Common insects today include salamanders.

B.

Write the missing word in each sentence.

1. There are perhaps ten _____ species of insects.
   (dozen, thousand, million)

2. All insects have _____ legs.
   (four, six, eight)

3. Eight out of every ten species of animals on Earth
   are _____ .
   (insects, amphibians, frogs)

4. It took _____ of years for amphibians to develop
   from fish.
   (hundreds, thousands, millions)

5. Amphibians live _____ of their lives in the water.
   (none, part, all)

C.

Write one or more sentences to answer the question.

Why might some kinds of fish have developed into the first amphibians?

_____

_____

_____

_____

4 What Are Reptiles?

Reptiles are vertebrate animals that have dry, scaly skin. Common reptiles include alligators, lizards, snakes, and turtles. Over millions of years, reptiles developed from amphibians.

There are two important differences between amphibians and reptiles. First, amphibians must lay their eggs in the water, but reptiles lay their eggs on land. This means that reptiles were the first vertebrates able to live their entire lives on land. Second, unlike amphibians, the tough, scaly skin on reptiles keeps them from drying out. They can live away from the shore. Over millions of years, reptiles spread out across the land.

The first reptiles appeared more than 280 million years ago. They were small and looked like salamanders. One of the earliest kinds of reptiles was the sailback. The sailback had huge fins, like sails, on its back. The fins may have helped the reptile control its body temperature. In hot weather, extra heat passed from the fin into the air. In cold weather, the fin collected heat from the air to warm the sailback's body. This helped it live in different climates.

As reptiles spread across the land, many different species of reptiles appeared. In time, reptiles of many shapes and sizes lived on the land. About 200 million years ago, two new kinds of reptiles developed. These included crocodiles that could live in water and pterosaurs. Pterosaurs were flying reptiles and were the first vertebrates that could fly.

Reptiles were one of the most successful groups of animals to roam Earth. For about 180 million years, they were the most important life form on Earth. For this reason, from about 245 million to about 65 million years ago is called The Age of Reptiles.

During The Age of Reptiles, many different kinds of reptiles roamed the land. Some were about the size of a chicken. Others were larger than elephants. Some lived on land, such as the sailback shown at the bottom of this picture. Some could swim and lived in the water. A few could fly, such as the pterosaurs shown at the top of this picture.

A. Write the missing word or words in each sentence.

1. Reptiles have _____.
   (wet skin, backbones, no backbones)

2. Reptiles developed from _____.
   (amphibians, insects, alligators)

3. Reptiles lay their eggs _____.
   (in the water, on land, anywhere)

4. The first reptiles looked like _____.
   (salamanders, insects, turtles)

5. The first flying reptiles were the _____.
   (crocodiles, sailbacks, pterosaurs)

6. The Age of Reptiles lasted about 180 _____ years.
   (thousand, million, billion)

B. Write <u>amphibians</u>, <u>reptiles</u>, or <u>both</u> to answer each question.

1. Which animals are vertebrates? _____

2. Which animals return to water to lay eggs? _____

3. Which animals lay eggs on land? _____

4. Which animals have tough, scaly skin that keeps them from drying out?

   _____

C. Write one or more sentences to answer the questions.

Imagine that both amphibians and reptiles live near a pond. Over many years, the pond fills with dirt until there is no water left. Which animals must move to find a new pond? Why?

_____

_____

_____

_____

What Are Dinosaurs and Birds?

Dinosaurs were reptiles that appeared about 230 million years ago. They ruled Earth for more than 140 million years. The smallest dinosaurs were about as big as chickens. The largest dinosaurs were the biggest land animals to ever live. Brachiosaurus, one of the largest dinosaurs, was 80 feet long and 40 feet tall. It weighed 80 tons!

Some dinosaurs, like the fierce tyrannosaurus, ate animals. Others, like stegosaurus, ate plants. Still others ate both plants and animals. Some dinosaurs ran on two legs; others walked on four. Some dinosaurs lived in groups or herds, while others lived alone.

About 65 million years ago, dinosaurs suddenly became extinct. Many scientists think the dinosaurs died when a huge meteorite crashed into Earth. The crash raised huge clouds of dust, blocking most of the sunlight. Without the sun, temperatures fell, and plants died. Dinosaurs that ate plants starved to death. Dinosaurs that ate animals also starved to death, because their prey had died.

It might surprise you to learn that birds developed from reptiles. Birds are feathered animals with wings. Today, there are nearly 9,000 species of birds in the world. Some of the earliest bird fossils are those of a bird called archaeopteryx, which appeared about 150 million years ago. The largest known archaeopteryx was the size of a crow. Like reptiles, it had teeth and a tail. Besides claws on its legs, it also had three reptile-like claws on each wing. It could glide and perhaps even fly, but not very well. The first modern birds appeared about 65 million years ago. Most of them were water birds. Fossils show birds with webbed feet that are good for swimming. Other birds, like the land birds we see today, developed slowly over millions of years.

There were many different kinds of dinosaurs. This picture shows some that ate plants—one stegosaurus and three ornithomimus.

Archaeopteryx had features of reptiles and birds. You can see feathers in this fossil of an archaeopteryx.

A.

Write **True** if the sentence is true. Write **False** if the sentence is false.

_____ 1. Dinosaurs were reptiles.

_____ 2. The smallest dinosaurs were as big as chickens.

_____ 3. The largest dinosaur was a tyrannosaurus.

_____ 4. All dinosaurs ate other animals.

_____ 5. Dinosaurs disappeared because their brains were too small for their bodies.

B.

Write the missing word or words in each sentence.

1. Dinosaurs were _____ that appeared about 230 million years ago.

    (amphibians, reptiles, birds)

2. Birds developed from _____ over millions of years.

    (ducks, flying insects, reptiles)

3. All birds have wings and _____.

    (feathers, teeth, claws on their wings)

4. One of the earliest birds was _____.

    (stegosaurus, archaeopteryx, brachiosaurus)

5. The first _____ appeared about 150 million years ago.

    (dinosaur, bird, reptile)

6. The largest of the first birds was the size of a _____.

    (small airplane, turkey, crow)

C.

Write one or more sentences to answer the question.

Why do you think so many people have found dinosaurs very interesting?

_____

_____

_____

6 What Are Mammals?

Mammals are vertebrates that feed their young with milk. Mammals have hair on their bodies. Also, mammals are more intelligent than many other animals. Today, there are about 4,500 species of mammals. Most familiar animals, like dogs, cats, and many farm animals, are mammals. Human beings are also mammals.

Like dinosaurs and birds, mammals developed from reptiles. Over many millions of years, some reptiles developed features that were mammal-like, such as special teeth. Scientists have found fossils of many of these mammal-like reptiles, such as some of the sailbacks.

Although mammals lived on Earth during The Age of Reptiles, they became widespread only after the dinosaurs became extinct, about 65 million years ago. Today, mammals rule Earth. This is why the time from the extinction of the dinosaurs to the present is called The Age of Mammals. Mammals have been successful because they have been able to **adapt**, or adjust, to life under many different conditions. An **adaptation** is a characteristic of an animal that helps it survive. For example, polar bears have adapted to life in a cold, snowy place. The adaptation of white fur hides them from their prey, and the adaptation of layers of fat keeps them warm.

Animals that do not adapt become extinct. Over millions of years, Earth has changed in many ways. Only species that developed the best adaptations survived these changes. This is why animal life on Earth has changed so much over time. This is true of the first water animals, fish, insects, amphibians, reptiles, and birds, as well as mammals.

What adaptations does the camel have for life in the desert?

What adaptation does the porcupine have to protect it from enemies?

A.

Put a ✔ next to each sentence that correctly describes mammals.

_____ 1. Mammals are invertebrates.

_____ 2. Mammals feed their young with milk.

_____ 3. Mammals have hair on their bodies.

_____ 4. Mammals include many familiar animals, as well as human beings.

_____ 5. Mammals became widespread before the dinosaurs became successful.

B.

Write the missing word or words in each sentence.

1. Mammals have been successful because they have adapted to

   _____.

   (different conditions, life on land, cold climates)

2. The time from about 65 million years ago to the present is known as The

   Age of _____.

   (Reptiles, Birds, Mammals)

3. An adaptation is a characteristic of an animal that helps it

   _____.

   (become extinct, survive, look better)

4. A polar bear's white fur is an example of _____.

   (a reptile-like quality, a poor color, an adaptation)

5. Animals that do not adapt _____.

   (lose weight, become extinct, need vitamins)

C.

Write one or more sentences to answer the question.

What adaptations do you think a deer has?

_____

_____

_____

Make a Model of a Fossil

You need:

- **gelatin cube**
- **seashell**
- **2 bowls**
- **modeling clay**
- **running water**

In this activity you will learn about fossils.

Follow these steps:

1. Roll out two flat pieces of clay the size of the bottom of each bowl.

2. Place the gelatin cube in one of the bowls. Place the seashell in the other bowl. Hold each bowl under running water for 30 seconds.

3. Place a flat piece of clay in the bottom of each bowl and press down gently.

4. Carefully remove the clay from each bowl.

Write answers to these questions.

1. What kind of animal does the gelatin cube represent? The seashell?

_____

_____

2. Which left a fossil in the clay? Why?

_____

_____

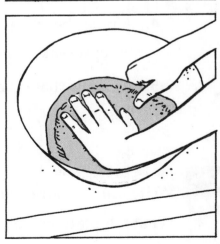

3. How could you model an animal with both hard and soft body parts?

_____

_____

Darken the circle next to the correct answer.

1. When did the first animal life appear on Earth?
   Ⓐ 600 million years ago
   Ⓑ 400 million years ago
   Ⓒ 250 million years ago
   Ⓓ 1 million years ago

2. The first animals lived
   Ⓐ only in the water.
   Ⓑ only on land.
   Ⓒ both in the water and on land.
   Ⓓ only in the air.

3. What were the first fish called?
   Ⓐ ostracoderms
   Ⓑ archaeopteryx
   Ⓒ sailbacks
   Ⓓ trilobites

4. A vertebrate is an animal that
   Ⓐ lives in the water.
   Ⓑ has no jaw.
   Ⓒ has a backbone.
   Ⓓ can fly.

5. Animals that live part of their lives in water and part on land are
   Ⓐ fish.
   Ⓑ insects.
   Ⓒ amphibians.
   Ⓓ mammals.

6. Reptiles developed from
   Ⓐ insects.
   Ⓑ birds.
   Ⓒ mammals.
   Ⓓ amphibians.

7. Which of these animals were reptiles?
   Ⓐ ostracoderms
   Ⓑ sailbacks
   Ⓒ trilobites
   Ⓓ archaeopteryx

8. What were dinosaurs?
   Ⓐ mammals
   Ⓑ amphibians
   Ⓒ reptiles
   Ⓓ insects

9. An example of a mammal is
   Ⓐ a human being.
   Ⓑ a turtle.
   Ⓒ a fish.
   Ⓓ an alligator.

10. An adaptation is a characteristic of an animal that helps it
    Ⓐ change.
    Ⓑ survive.
    Ⓒ look better.
    Ⓓ become extinct.

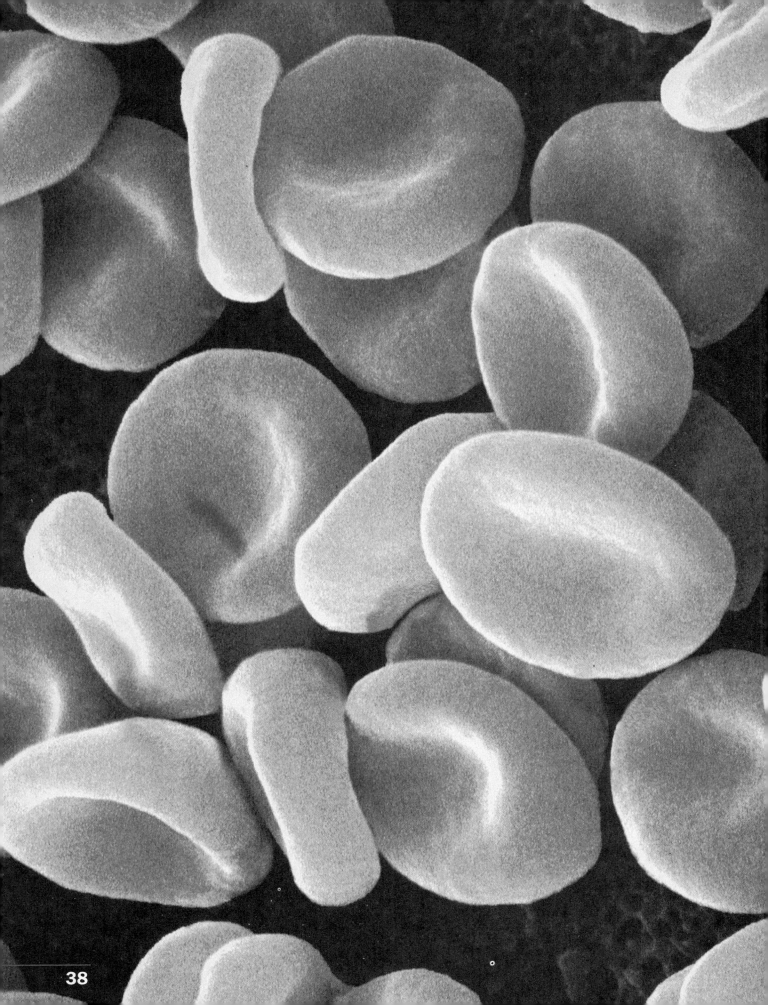

CHAPTER

3

Body Systems

Your body is made of many parts that do many jobs. Your bones give shape to your body. Muscles let you move. Your lungs let you breathe. Your digestive system turns food into fuel. Some parts of your blood carry food or fight sickness. The job of the red blood cells shown in the picture is to carry oxygen to all the parts of your body. Red blood cells also carry away waste carbon dioxide that body cells do not need.

What is it?

- It has a hard outer layer and a soft inner layer.
- It is moved by muscles.
- It is connected to others like itself at joints.

What Is Your Skeletal System?

Your skeleton gives shape and support to your body. Your skeleton allows you to sit and stand, to walk and run. The skeleton is made of **bones** and moved by **muscles**.

Bones like the skull and backbone have very special purposes, but every bone plays a part in supporting you and protecting your insides. Each bone has a hard outer layer and a soft inner layer. Some bones are tiny, like those in your hands and feet. Others are much larger, like those in your thighs. The average adult has about 200 bones.

The bones in your skeleton are connected at **joints**. There are several kinds of joints. For example, finger joints work like the hinge on a door. Hip joints work like a ball moving inside a round cup. Soft, and sometimes elastic, tissues hold joints like those in your spine in place. They cushion bones as the joints move.

Muscles allow you to move your bones. They are attached to the bones by elastic tissues called **tendons**. Muscles work in pairs. When one contracts, or tightens, the other relaxes. To bend your arm, the muscle at the front of your arm tightens as its partner at the back of your arm relaxes.

The muscles that move your skeleton are **voluntary muscles** because you can move them when you want to. They are made of long bands of tissue held together like many rubber bands. Other muscles make up the group of **involuntary muscles**. These muscles, which include those in your eyes and stomach, contract and relax without your control. This allows you to breathe and digest your food, for example, even while sleeping. Involuntary muscles are also called smooth muscles because they are made of smooth tissues.

The Human Skeleton

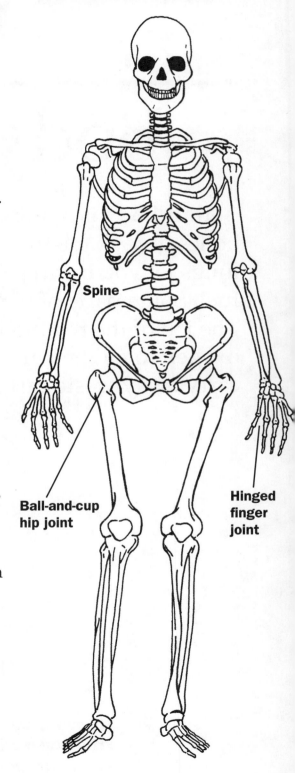

Spine

Ball-and-cup hip joint

Hinged finger joint

40

A. Write the missing word or words in each sentence.

1. Bones make up your skeleton, and _____ move your skeleton.

   (muscles, the eyes, the backbones)

2. Besides supporting you, your bones _____ the insides of your body.

   (relax, protect, heat)

3. Your bones are connected at _____.

   (voluntary muscles, the tendons, joints)

4. Elastic tissues called _____ attach your muscles to your bones.

   (joints, smooth muscles, tendons)

5. To move a part of the body, one muscle tightens and its partner

   _____.

   (contracts, relaxes, cushions)

B. Write V if the sentence tells about voluntary muscles. Write I if the sentence tells about involuntary muscles.

_____ 1. They relax when you choose to relax them.

_____ 2. They are made of smooth tissues.

_____ 3. They contract without your control.

_____ 4. They are made of long bands of tissue.

C. Write one or more sentences to answer the questions.

If you tore a tendon in your knee joint, would the joint still work correctly? Why or why not?

_____

_____

_____

_____

What Is Blood?

Your **blood** is made of **plasma**, **red blood cells**, **white blood cells**, and **platelets**. Each part of your blood has a different job.

Plasma is a yellow liquid made mostly of water. It acts as a stream in which the red blood cells, white blood cells, and platelets float. It also carries food to your body's other cells and helps you stay evenly warm from your head to your toes.

Red blood cells carry oxygen from the air you breathe to all the parts of your body. When they reach their destination, the red blood cells leave the oxygen for body cells to use. Then, they pick up **carbon dioxide**, or waste gas, that body cells do not need. They take this to the lungs, where you breathe it out. When red blood cells are full of oxygen, they are bright red. When they carry carbon dioxide, they are dark red.

White blood cells act as the body's soldiers against disease. Some white blood cells quickly attack germs by eating them. Other smaller white blood cells can move out of the blood to reach body tissues. When you cut yourself or breathe in germs, your body makes many more white cells to fight the germs. Both kinds of white blood cells move to where the germs are and work together to destroy them. White blood cells then carry the dead germs and any dead body cells away.

Platelets allow your blood to clot, or thicken and clump together, around a cut. They also help repair the blood system by closing any holes. Platelets are the smallest of the blood cells and are very sticky. They create a web of sticky threads around red blood cells and around each other. This web makes a plug to close the hole made by a cut or wound. Platelets, like both red and white blood cells, are made deep inside the bones.

Parts of the Blood

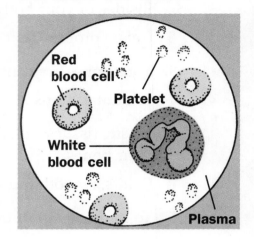

Red blood cell

Platelet

White blood cell

Plasma

A.

Draw a line to match the part of the blood to the job it does in the body.

1. Red blood cells   kill germs to fight disease.

2. White blood cells   clot blood to close wounds.

3. Platelets   carry oxygen to body cells.

B.

Write the word or words that best complete each sentence.

| body | carbon dioxide | platelets | white blood cells |
| bones | plasma | water | |

1. Blood is made mainly of red blood cells, white blood cells, platelets, and

   _____.

2. Plasma helps the _____ stay warm.

3. Plasma is made mostly of _____.

4. Red blood cells pick up _____ and take it back to the lungs.

5. When cells die at a wound or from disease, _____ carry them away.

6. Sticky threads made by _____ help close up holes made by cuts or wounds.

7. The body makes blood cells inside the _____.

C.

Write one or more sentences to answer the question.

How do white blood cells and platelets work together to protect the body when it is wounded?

_____

_____

_____

_____

_____

LESSON 3

What Is Your Circulatory System?

To do its many jobs, the blood must travel throughout your body. The blood moves from the **heart** to all parts of your body and then back to the heart again. **Blood vessels** are the tubes through which blood travels. Together, the blood, the heart, and blood vessels are the three main parts of a system. Because it is like a circle, this system is called your **circulatory system**.

The heart is a special muscle that pumps blood throughout the body. The heart has two sides, each with its own pump. The left side pumps blood filled with oxygen out into the body for cells to use. The blood returns to the heart's right side without oxygen and filled with carbon dioxide. The heart's right side pumps this blood to your lungs. In the lungs, the carbon dioxide leaves the blood. Then, the blood collects more oxygen from the air you breathe. The blood, filled with oxygen, returns to the heart. It flows into the heart's left side and is once again pumped out into the body.

All the blood pumped by the heart travels through blood vessels. There are three main kinds of blood vessels—**arteries**, **veins**, and **capillaries**.

Arteries carry blood that contains oxygen. This blood travels through smaller and smaller arteries to reach body cells. Finally, it reaches very tiny tubes called **capillaries**. This is where the exchange of oxygen and carbon dioxide happens. Blood containing carbon dioxide flows on through the capillaries into small **veins**. Veins are the blood vessels that carry blood containing carbon dioxide. The blood now moves through larger and larger veins to reach the heart. It enters the heart's right side. The blood is pumped to the lungs for more oxygen and the circle repeats again.

The Circulatory System

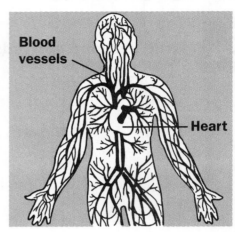

The Heart

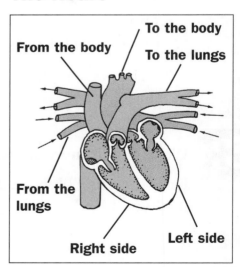

A. Write the missing word or words in each sentence.

1. The three main parts of the circulatory system are the blood, the heart,

   and _____.

   (platelets, tendons, blood vessels)

2. The heart is a special _____ that pumps blood
   throughout the body.

   (bone, tendon, muscle)

3. Blood returning to the heart from body cells is filled

   with _____.

   (oxygen, carbon dioxide, veins)

4. Arteries carry blood that contains _____.

   (oxygen, carbon dioxide, veins)

5. The exchange of oxygen and carbon dioxide takes place in blood vessels

   called _____.

   (arteries, veins, capillaries)

B. The sentences below tell how blood circulates through the heart and lungs. Write 1, 2, 3, 4, and 5 to show the correct order. The first one is done for you.

_____ Carbon dioxide is exchanged for oxygen in the lungs.

_____ The heart's left side pumps blood containing oxygen out to the body.

_____ The heart's right side pumps blood to the lungs.

_____ Blood filled with oxygen returns to the heart and enters the left side.

____1____ Blood filled with carbon dioxide enters the heart's right side from
veins.

C. Write one or more sentences to answer the questions.

Do you think that the heart is a voluntary muscle or an involuntary muscle?
Why?

_____

_____

What Is Your Respiratory System?

Like most living things, you need oxygen to live. Your body gets oxygen when you breathe. Carbon dioxide is removed when you breathe. Breathing takes place in your **respiratory system**. The respiratory system includes the **trachea**, **lungs**, and **diaphragm**.

The **trachea** is the main air pipe, leading from your nose and mouth to your lungs. Also called the windpipe, it is found in your throat and neck. Air enters your body through your nose and mouth. The lining in the nose removes dirt from the air. It also warms the air and makes it less dry. The trachea leads into the chest to your lungs. A flap at the top of the trachea keeps out food and other objects. The trachea divides into two main tubes, one leading to each lung. Inside the lungs, these tubes divide into smaller and smaller tubes.

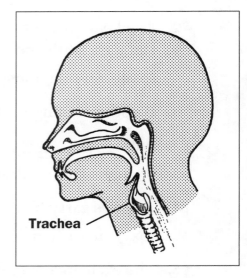

The trachea is the main air pipe, leading from your nose and mouth to your lungs.

The **lungs** are where the exchange of oxygen and carbon dioxide takes place. The smallest branches of your air pipes connect to bunches of tiny air sacs. In the walls of these sacs are capillaries. When you breathe in, air filled with oxygen collects in the air sacs. The oxygen passes through the very thin walls of the capillaries into your blood. Carbon dioxide passes back through the capillary walls into the air sacs. When you breathe out, carbon dioxide travels back through the system of air pipes and out your nose or mouth.

To make space for the air you breathe in, your chest must get larger. An involuntary muscle called the **diaphragm** works with your chest muscles to do this. The diaphragm is a smooth muscle stretched across the bottom of your lungs. When it contracts, it gets flatter and pulls the lungs down. Your chest muscles pull your ribs up and out. As the space inside your chest grows, air is sucked in and the elastic lungs grow larger. When you breathe out, the muscles relax and the lungs shrink.

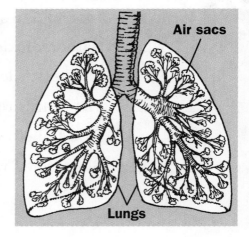

The exchange of oxygen and carbon dioxide takes place in the lungs.

A.

Write the word or words that best complete each sentence.

| air sacs | diaphragm | nose |
| capillaries | lungs | trachea |

Air enters the body at the _____ or mouth. It travels through the _____ down into the chest. Air then flows into one of two tubes into the _____. Here, air flows through smaller and smaller tubes to reach tiny _____. The exchange of oxygen and carbon dioxide takes place when these gases pass through the thin walls of _____. To make space for the air inside the chest, an involuntary muscle called the _____ gets flatter, pulling the lungs down.

B.

Label the picture with the correct name for each part of the respiratory system.

| diaphragm | lungs | trachea |

C.

Write one or more sentences to answer the questions.

If a piece of food got into your trachea, what might happen? Would you still be able to breathe? Why or why not?

_____

_____

5 What Is Your Digestive System?

Along with oxygen, you need food to stay alive. Your **digestive system** turns the food you eat into fuel. This fuel runs your body's systems. It gives you energy. It also helps you grow and stay healthy.

The digestive system is a long tube with many folds that passes through several body parts. Three of these parts are the mouth, the **stomach**, and the **intestines**. Each part works differently to break down food into smaller and smaller pieces. The tiniest pieces then enter the blood.

Food enters the system through your mouth. You chew and grind with your teeth to break it down. Your mouth makes **saliva**. This liquid softens food before it passes into your **esophagus**. The esophagus is the tube leading from your mouth to your stomach. It is made of rings of involuntary muscle. These muscles push food down into the stomach.

The stomach stores food. Stomach muscles mix the food with special chemicals. These chemicals break down the food even further. Some kinds of food pass quickly through the stomach. Others remain in the stomach longer because they take longer to break down.

Food passes from the stomach into the small intestine. The small intestine is a very long tube that is coiled, or folded. Food is pushed slowly through this intestine by muscles like those in the esophagus. Chemicals in the small intestine finish breaking down the food. The walls of the intestine soak up tiny pieces of food. This food enters your blood through blood vessels in the intestine's walls. Any food that cannot be used passes into the large intestine. The large intestine is not as long as the small intestine, but it is bigger around. The large intestine draws water out of this food. The matter that remains leaves the body as solid waste.

The Digestive System

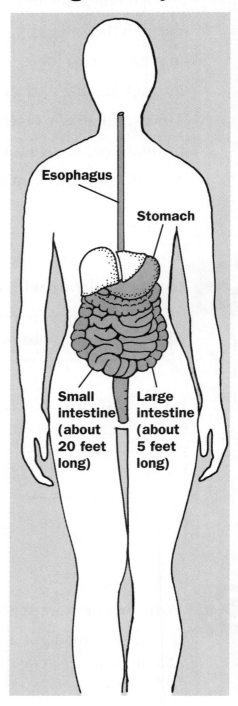

Esophagus

Stomach

Small intestine (about 20 feet long)

Large intestine (about 5 feet long)

A.

Write 1, 2, 3, 4, and 5 to show the order in which food passes through the digestive system. The first one is done for you.

_____ large intestine

_____ stomach

____1____ mouth

_____ esophagus

_____ small intestine

B.

Write the missing word or words in each sentence.

1. The digestive system gets energy from _____.
   (air, food, blood)

2. Three important parts of the digestive system are the esophagus, the
   intestines, and the _____.
   (stomach, lungs, trachea)

3. In the mouth, food is mixed with _____ to soften it.
   (water, saliva, carbon dioxide)

4. Food is pushed through the esophagus by rings of
   _____.
   (involuntary muscle, small intestine, capillaries)

5. The stomach _____ food and also breaks it down
   with chemicals.
   (chews, makes, stores)

6. Food pieces pass into the blood through the walls of the
   _____.
   (large intestine, small intestine, stomach)

C.

Write one or more sentences to answer the question.

How would your digestive system act if your involuntary muscles stopped working?

_____

_____

6 What Is Your Excretory System?

Like a car, your body cannot use all the material it takes in for fuel. Some parts of the material may be harmful. Others may be useless to the body. Also, actions like running and eating make waste that the body cannot use or store. This waste is passed out of the body through the **excretory system**. Three important parts of this system are the **kidneys**, the lungs, and the skin.

The two kidneys are found near the lower back. Shaped like beans but much larger, the kidneys remove waste from your blood. Blood flows into the kidneys to tiny capsules. There, the blood is cleaned. Waste chemicals and water are taken out of the blood. The cleaned blood passes out of the kidneys, back into the main blood system. The waste liquid goes to the **bladder**. It is stored in this sack until it can leave the body.

The lungs remove waste in several ways. They catch and breathe out pieces of dust or dirt from the air you breathe. The lungs also collect carbon dioxide made when the body uses oxygen. That carbon dioxide passes into the air sacs of the lungs during breathing. The lungs remove carbon dioxide when you breathe out. Finally, the lungs remove a little bit of extra water from your body. This water is in such tiny amounts that you cannot usually see it. Sometimes on a cold day, however, a little cloud will form when you breathe out. This is the water in your breath turned to mist by cold outside air.

Waste water and chemicals can also leave the body through tiny holes in your skin. This is called sweating. You sweat more when your body gets very warm from exercise, hot weather, or illness. The skin also sheds waste in the form of dead cells. New skin cells form all the time to replace those that are shed.

The Excretory System

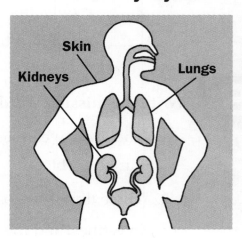

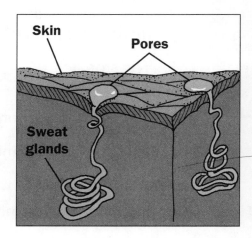

Sweat glands pass waste water and chemicals out of the body through pores in the skin.

A. Write <u>True</u> if the sentence is true. Write <u>False</u> if the sentence is false.

_____ 1. Kidneys remove waste by cleaning pieces of dust out of the air you breathe.

_____ 2. Carbon dioxide waste is removed from the body by the lungs.

_____ 3. The lungs, skin, and kidneys can remove waste water from the body.

B. Write the missing word or words in each sentence.

1. The three important parts of the excretory system are the kidneys, the lungs, and the _____.

   (bones, muscles, skin)

2. Waste from the kidneys is stored in the _____.

   (lungs, blood, bladder)

3. The skin sheds waste in the form of sweat and

   _____.

   (cleaned blood, oxygen, dead cells)

C. Draw a line to complete each sentence.

1. Waste   is stored in the bladder.

2. Blood   sheds waste through tiny holes.

3. Waste liquid   is cleaned in tiny capsules inside the kidneys.

4. Skin   is made by the body as it works.

D. Write one or more sentences to answer the question.

Why is it important to the kidneys for a person to drink at least eight glasses of water a day?

_____

_____

CHAPTER 3

Make a Model of a Lung

You need:

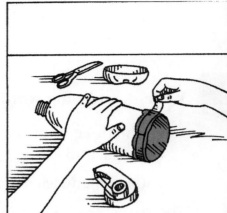

- **safety goggles**
- **1-liter soda bottle**
- **scissors**
- **large balloon**
- **small balloon**
- **drinking straw**
- **tape**
- **modeling clay**

In this activity you will see how your lungs work.

Follow these steps:

1. Put on your goggles. Carefully cut the bottom off the soda bottle. Then, cut the neck off the large balloon.

2. Stretch the large balloon across the large end of the bottle. Seal it with tape. Stretch the neck of the small balloon around one end of the drinking straw. Seal it with tape.

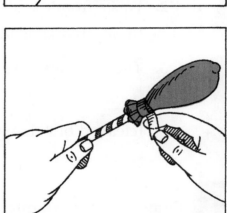

3. Place the straw in the neck of the bottle. Use the clay to seal the straw in place.

4. Pinch the middle of the large balloon between your fingertips and pull it out. Write what you see. Press in on the large balloon. Write what you see.

Write answers to these questions.

1. What part of your body does the large balloon represent? The small balloon?

   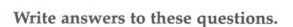

   _____

2. What were you modeling when you pulled out the balloon? When you pushed in the balloon?

   _____

Darken the circle next to the correct answer.

1. Bones, muscles, and joints are part of your
   Ⓐ skeletal system.
   Ⓑ tendons.
   Ⓒ involuntary system.
   Ⓓ stomach.

2. Which blood cells carry oxygen to all the parts of your body?
   Ⓐ plasma
   Ⓑ red blood cells
   Ⓒ white blood cells
   Ⓓ platelets

3. Which blood cells attack germs?
   Ⓐ plasma
   Ⓑ red blood cells
   Ⓒ white blood cells
   Ⓓ platelets

4. Blood moves from arteries to veins through tiny tubes called
   Ⓐ pumps.
   Ⓑ capillaries.
   Ⓒ germs.
   Ⓓ lungs.

5. Blood traveling from the heart to the lungs is filled with
   Ⓐ oxygen.
   Ⓑ oxygen and carbon dioxide.
   Ⓒ carbon dioxide.
   Ⓓ air.

6. During breathing, the exchange of oxygen and carbon dioxide takes place in the
   Ⓐ lungs.
   Ⓑ diaphragm.
   Ⓒ trachea.
   Ⓓ windpipe.

7. What makes the lungs grow bigger to make space for new air?
   Ⓐ capillaries
   Ⓑ air sacs
   Ⓒ diaphragm
   Ⓓ carbon dioxide

8. The large intestine helps digest food by
   Ⓐ soaking small pieces into its lining.
   Ⓑ grinding food with teeth.
   Ⓒ storing food.
   Ⓓ drawing water out of food.

9. Which body system turns food into energy for the body's work?
   Ⓐ circulatory
   Ⓑ digestive
   Ⓒ respiratory
   Ⓓ excretory

10. The three body parts that help remove waste from the body are
    Ⓐ tendons, kidneys, and bladder.
    Ⓑ bladder, skin, and lower back.
    Ⓒ lungs, kidneys, and tendons.
    Ⓓ skin, lungs, and kidneys.

Careers

Botanist

A botanist is a scientist who studies plants. There are many different kinds of plants that a botanist might study—more than 350,000! When a new plant is discovered, a botanist names it and decides what kind of plants it is most like.

Some botanists use what they learn about plants to help people. Some botanists develop ways to grow more or better crops. Other botanists find ways to use plants as medicine. Still other botanists suggest ways to protect the places where plants grow in the wild.

Herpetologist

Herpeton means crawling thing. But the animals that a herpetologist studies do much more than crawl. Some of them walk, slither, and hop!

Herpetologists study reptiles like snakes, lizards, and crocodiles. They also study amphibians like frogs and salamanders. Herpetologists watch these animals to learn what they eat, how they move, how they change, and how they raise their young.

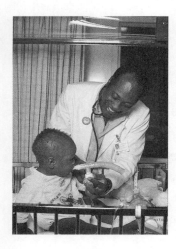

Respiratory Therapist

People cannot live without breathing. When someone is having trouble breathing, a respiratory therapist can help.

Respiratory therapists work with doctors in hospitals. Respiratory therapists use machines called **respirators** to help people breathe. They also test respirators and order repairs. Sometimes respiratory therapists teach people exercises to help them breathe better.

Unit 2

Earth Science

The land may be flat, hilly, or mountainous. Air temperatures may change often or hardly at all. Perhaps lots of rain or snow falls. But there are windmills like these only in places that have fairly steady winds. Windmills turn wind energy into electrical power. In this unit you'll learn about the characteristics of different places on Earth.

CHAPTER 4

Biomes

This camel lives where there are few trees. The soil is sandy and full of gravel. There is little rain, and water is probably hard to find. Camels do well in this environment. Scientists say they are adapted to their climate. The camel's feet are broad and flat, so they don't sink into the sand. Thick eyebrows shade the camel's eyes, and long eyelashes keep out blowing sand. In this chapter you'll learn about the types of environments on Earth and the adaptations of plants and animals that live in them.

What is it?

- Trees need it to grow.
- It is scarce in the tundra and in the desert.
- It falls to Earth.

What Is a Biome?

Do you ever wonder why there is so much diversity, or so many different plants and animals living on our planet? Plants and animals live on frozen grasslands and in sizzling deserts. Plants and animals live where rain falls every day and where rain may not fall for years. There is great diversity among plants and animals because there is great diversity among the places where they live.

Special temperature and rainfall patterns form the **climate** of an area. The climate makes life possible for particular plants. The plants make life possible for particular animals. A large place with a certain climate and plants and animals suited to that climate is called a **biome**. There are desert biomes and forest biomes. There are grassland biomes. Furthermore, the same biomes are found in different parts of the world. For example, there are grassland biomes on almost every continent on Earth. But you may be surprised to learn that the plants and animals that live in these grassland biomes are not always the same.

Let's use two grasslands as examples of how diverse plants and animals can live in the same biomes. In North America, the climate in part of the middle of the continent supports grasslands. You can see grasses and animals such as hawks and prairie dogs. In Africa, the climate in the middle of the continent supports another kind of grassland called a **savanna**. Grasses grow here, too, but zebras and giraffes graze on these grasses.

A biome, then, is a large area with a certain climate. Different plants and animals have adapted to life in each biome. And even when the same biome appears on different continents, the plants and animals that live in that biome are different.

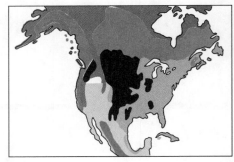

	Tundra
	Taiga
	Deciduous forest
	Grassland
	Desert

This map shows different biomes in North America.

A. Write the missing word or words in each sentence.

1. Special temperature and rainfall patterns form the

   _____ of an area.

   (diversity, biome, climate)

2. A large place with a certain climate and particular plants and animals

   is called a _____.

   (savanna, biome, continent)

3. In the same kind of biome in two different parts of the world, the

   _____ always the same.

   (plants are, animals are, climate is)

4. In Africa, zebras and giraffes graze on grasses on the

   _____.

   (savanna, climate, biome)

B. Write **True** if the sentence is true. Write **False** if the sentence is false.

_____ 1. All biomes have the same climate.

_____ 2. The same plants can live in all biomes.

_____ 3. A biome's climate determines what can live there.

_____ 4. Biomes that are alike can be found in different parts of the world.

_____ 5. Animals are not adapted to living in cold biomes.

_____ 6. Some plants are adapted to living in dry biomes.

C. Write one or more sentences to answer the question.

If just one biome covered Earth, what do you think would be true of the plants and animals that live there?

_____

_____

_____

_____

2 What Are the Tundra and the Taiga?

The two coldest biomes are the **tundra** and the **taiga**. For most of the year, the tundra is a frozen grassland. There is little **precipitation**, or rain and snow, that falls. Below the surface, the soil is always frozen. Strong, dry winds, frozen soil, and little precipitation keep trees from growing on the tundra. But for a short time during the summer, the tundra warms, and the snow and ice near the surface of the ground melt. Tundra plants bloom and grow before the water freezes again.

A polar bear's thick fur coat protects it from the cold of the tundra.

Many kinds of geese and ducks live on the tundra during the short summer. There they feed on the huge numbers of insects that hatch. The birds fly south when temperatures get colder. Some of the larger tundra animals, such as reindeer, also travel south in great herds to forests that protect them from the cold. Other animals, such as polar bears, arctic hares, arctic foxes, and lemmings, live on the tundra all year. They have thick fur coats that help protect them from the cold.

The **taiga** is a large forest that has a warmer climate than the tundra, but the summers remain short and the winters long. There is more precipitation, too, but snow covers the ground throughout the winter. Unlike the tundra, the taiga has many trees. Most of the trees stay green all year, so they are called **evergreens**. Spruce and fir trees are two kinds of evergreens that grow in the taiga. Their leaves are narrow and pointed, like needles. The leaves have a coating that protects them from the cold.

With the trees to provide food and shelter, more kinds of animals can live in the taiga than on the tundra. Small animals, such as snowshoe hares and birds, feed on the seeds of the evergreens. The trees also give them shelter. The trees protect large taiga animals, too, such as elk, moose, and bears.

A. Write the word or words that best complete each sentence.

arctic hare	reindeer	taiga
evergreens	spruce	tundra

1. Trees cannot grow on the _____.

2. Some tundra animals, such as _____, go south for the winter.

3. Some tundra animals, such as the _____, live on the tundra throughout the year.

4. Many trees grow in the _____.

5. Trees that stay green all year are called _____.

6. In the taiga, two common evergreens are fir and

   _____.

B. Write the word tundra or taiga to tell where each plant or animal can be found.

1. polar bear _____

2. arctic fox _____

3. lemmings _____

4. spruce _____

5. elk _____

C. Write one or more sentences to answer the question.

Why do you think the arctic hare's coat changes color from white in winter to brown or gray in summer?

_____

_____

_____

_____

What Are Deserts?

Deserts are the driest biomes. They receive less than ten inches of rain in a year. Some deserts may get no rain at all for a year, or even longer. With so little rain, you might think that deserts are covered with only sand for miles and miles. Some deserts are like this, but most deserts have many kinds of plant and animal life. All plants and animals need some water to live, so desert plants and animals have special adaptations, or characteristics, for living in the desert.

Some desert plants have very long roots that can reach water far underground. Desert plants like cactus plants have waxy coverings on their stems and leaves that help them keep water. Some desert plants grow only when it rains. When rain falls, these plants grow very fast and make many flowers and seeds. After a single rainfall, these plants suddenly turn the brown desert floor into a carpet of colors.

Animals also have different ways of living in a hot, dry place. Like some cactus plants, some insects have a waxy coating on their bodies. The coating keeps the insects from drying out. Many desert animals spend the hottest part of the day in holes in the ground or under the shade of rocks, where they are protected from the heat. They come out to feed at night when it is much cooler. Some animals, like kangaroo rats and desert foxes, have large ears filled with tiny blood vessels that help the animals lose extra body heat.

The camel is the largest desert animal. It has large, flat feet with thick pads that help it walk on hot sand. One kind of camel has one hump on its back. Another kind has two humps. Camels store fat in these humps. The fat helps block the flow of heat into the camel's body. Camels lose water from their bodies slowly. They can live as much as a week in summer and even longer in winter without water.

Cactus plants have spines to protect them from animals that try to get water from inside the plants.

Camels do not store water in the humps on their backs. They drink as much as 25 gallons of water at a time. Then, camels lose water very slowly from their bodies.

Write <u>True</u> if the sentence is true. Write <u>False</u> if the sentence is false.

_____ 1. Deserts often get more than 20 inches of rain a year.

_____ 2. Some animals don't need water to live.

_____ 3. Some desert plants grow only when it rains.

_____ 4. Some desert animals come out at night when it is cooler.

_____ 5. Camels store water in the humps on their backs.

B. Write the word that best completes each sentence.

adaptations	deserts	night
cactus	ears	underground

1. The driest biomes are _____.

2. Desert plants and animals have special _____, or characteristics, that help them live in the desert.

3. Desert plants like the _____ have a waxy coating to hold in water.

4. Many desert animals spend the hottest hours in

_____ holes to keep cool.

5. Many desert animals feed at _____ to keep cool.

6. Some desert animals have large _____ that help them lose body heat.

C. Write one or more sentences to answer the question.

Why do you think the desert plants that live only briefly when it rains make many seeds?

_____

_____

_____

_____

4 What Are Grasslands?

Grasslands don't have many hiding places, so some small grassland animals such as gophers escape to underground burrows for safety.

Grasslands are dry biomes that get more rain than deserts, but not enough steady rain for many trees to grow. Grasslands in the United States usually receive ten to thirty inches of rain each year.

Grasslands cover large areas of many parts of the world. Just as this biome's name tells you, the main plants of a grassland are different kinds of grasses. Grasslands are home to many animals, called grazing animals, that depend on grass for food. Bison, antelopes, and kangaroos are grazing animals. Grazing animals often travel through grasslands in large groups called herds. Many plant-eating insects live in grasslands. Many birds who feed on insects and seeds live there, too.

Since there are few trees or bushes, grasslands don't have many places for animals to hide from their enemies. So many grassland animals, such as gazelles, are very fast runners. Some small grassland animals, such as gophers, escape to underground homes called **burrows**.

In some parts of the world, such as Africa and Australia, grasslands have two seasons—a dry season and a wet season. During the dry season, the grass is shorter and turns brown, and it becomes even harder for animals to hide. For this reason, many grassland animals, such as the puff adder snake, are a brown color that matches the color of the dry brown grasses. This protects them, because animals that try to hunt them for food can't see them easily.

The grassland biome covers one third of the United States, where much of it has been turned into farmland. The wetter grasslands are good for growing corn and wheat, while cows and sheep can graze on the drier grasslands.

A. Write the word or words that best complete each sentence.

burrows	grasslands	herd	wheat
dry season	grazing animals	one-third	

1. Although it is too dry for trees to grow there, _____ get more rain than deserts.

2. Animals that depend on grass for food are called

   _____.

3. Sometimes antelopes travel in a large group called a

   _____.

4. Gophers hide in underground holes called _____.

5. The grassland turns brown during the _____.

6. The grassland that covers _____ of the United States is used for farming.

7. Two important crops grown on grasslands are corn and

   _____.

B. Match each plant or animal with the words that name an adaptation for living in the grassland.

1. gazelle   escapes to underground burrow

2. gopher   color matches dry grasses

3. puff adder snake   very fast runner

C. Write one or more sentences to answer the question.

Why might grazing animals travel in herds?

_____

_____

_____

5 What Are Forests?

Forests are biomes that have many trees growing close together. There are many kinds of forests. Temperature and rainfall determine the kind of forest that grows.

Trees that lose their leaves in autumn and grow new ones every spring are called **deciduous** trees. Maple and oak trees are deciduous trees. Forests with many of these kinds of trees are called deciduous forests. Deciduous forests are home to many plants and animals. Woodpeckers and other birds live in the trees and feed on insects, seeds, and fruit. Many smaller plants, such as shrubs, wildflowers, and ferns, grow among the trees. Mosses and fallen seeds and fruit are on the forest floor where mice, foxes, deer, and many other animals live.

Rain forests are forest biomes that receive from 80 to 200 or more inches of rain each year. Rain forests are usually found where temperatures are warm all year. These parts of the world are called the **tropics**. Forests that grow there are called tropical rain forests.

Tropical rain forests are home to more kinds of plants and animals than any other biome on Earth. Because the wet, warm climate makes it a perfect place for plants to grow, rain forests are thick with plant life. The forest is crowded with trees that grow tall to reach light. Their branches spread out, forming a roof of leaves, vines, and flowers over the forest. This roof, or top part of the rain forest, is called the **canopy**.

A variety of animal life is found in the canopy of the rain forest. There are great numbers of animals that cling and climb, such as insects, birds, tree frogs, tree snakes, fruit bats, monkeys, and sloths. Many other animals, such as anteaters and wild pigs, live on the forest floor.

Monkeys and many other climbing animals live in the canopy of the rain forest and feed on the plentiful leaves and fruits there.

A. Write the missing word or words in each sentence.

1. The kind of forest that grows in an area is determined by temperature and

   _____.

   (canopy, rainfall, insects)

2. Trees that lose their leaves in autumn are called

   _____.

   (hybrids, evergreen, deciduous)

3. Biomes that receive 80 to 200 inches of rain a year are

   _____.

   (rain forests, taiga, wetlands)

4. The treetops of the rain forest make up the _____.
   (canopy, tropics, top floor)

5. In the rain forest, many climbing animals, such as monkeys, live in

   _____.

   (grasslands, the canopy, burrows)

B. Write R for rain forest or D for deciduous forest to show which kind of forest is being described.

_____ 1. The trees lose their leaves in autumn.

_____ 2. It is usually found in the tropics.

_____ 3. It is home to the most kinds of plants and animals.

_____ 4. Many animals live in its canopy.

C. Write one or more sentences to answer the question.

How does the climate of the tropical rain forest make it a good home for many kinds of animals?

_____

_____

_____

LESSON 6

What Are Aquatic Biomes?

This lantern fish lives deep in the marine biome. Like all fish, it uses gills to take oxygen from the water. It is called a lantern fish because it glows like a lantern to attract prey and to communicate with other lantern fish.

You have learned about land biomes with different climates and about the plants and animals that live in them. But what about areas where plants and animals live in water? These are called **aquatic biomes**. There are two main kinds of aquatic biomes—**saltwater** and freshwater. Saltwater biomes, or **marine biomes**, include all the oceans of the world. Oceans cover three fourths of Earth.

Plants that grow in marine biomes need sunlight for photosynthesis. They grow on or near the surface of the water, where light reaches. Some of the plants in marine biomes, such as seaweeds, can be large enough to make underwater forests. Other kinds of plants are very small and float at the surface of the ocean. These tiny plants are called **plankton**. Thousands of them might be found in a cup of ocean water. Some tiny animals are called plankton, too. Plankton are important to all ocean life, because many small fish eat the plankton, and then many kinds of larger fish eat the small fish.

Marine biomes are also home to many kinds of creatures, from tiny shrimp to the blue whale. There are fish of all shapes and sizes. All of these animals need oxygen to live. Some of them, such as whales, get oxygen by swimming to the surface and taking breaths. Others, such as fish and shrimp, take in oxygen from the water around them through special body parts called **gills**.

The other main kind of aquatic biome is the freshwater biome. It includes lakes, ponds, rivers, and streams. Freshwater biomes have little or no salt. They are also home to many kinds of plant and animal life. Freshwater plants grow where sunlight reaches them. And the animals get oxygen in the same ways as the animals that live in marine biomes.

A.

Write the word or words that best complete each sentence.

aquatic biomes	**gills**	**oxygen**
freshwater biomes	**marine biomes**	**plankton**

1. Areas where plants and animals live in water are called

   _____.

2. Earth's oceans make up the _____.

3. Tiny, floating plants and animals called _____ live
   in the marine biome.

4. Animals that live in aquatic biomes need to breathe

   _____.

5. Biomes with little or no salt in the water are known as

   _____.

6. Fish in aquatic biomes take in oxygen through their

   _____.

B.

Write <u>Marine</u> if the sentence describes a saltwater biome. Write <u>Freshwater</u> if
the sentence describes a freshwater biome.

1. It covers three fourths of Earth.   _____

2. The water contains much salt.   _____

3. It includes lakes and ponds.   _____

4. Little salt is in the water.   _____

C.

Write one or more sentences to answer the question.

Brook trout is a kind of fish that lives in a freshwater biome. If you put a brook
trout in a marine biome, it will die. Why do you think that is?

_____

_____

Make a Rainfall Gauge

You need:

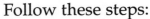

- **coffee can or large juice can**
- **inch ruler**   • **tape**   • **paper**   • **pencil**

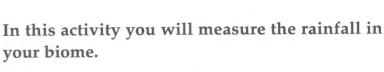

In this activity you will measure the rainfall in your biome.

Follow these steps:

1. Place the ruler inside the can. The end of the ruler before the 1-inch mark should be at the bottom of the can. Tape the ruler in place.

2. Place your rainfall gauge outside in a place where it won't be disturbed or blown over.

3. Make a "Rainfall Log" like the one in the picture. Leave spaces to enter the rainfall each day for the next week.

4. Check your rainfall gauge each day. Record the amount of rain shown on the ruler. Empty the rainfall gauge after you take your reading.

Rainfall Log	
Day	Rainfall
Day 1	1¼ inches
Day 2	
Day 3	

Write answers to these questions.

1. On which day did it rain the most? What was the amount?

   _____

2. On which day did it rain the least? What was the amount?

   _____

3. How does the rainfall in your area affect living things in your biome?

   _____

   _____

Darken the circle next to the correct answer.

1. A large area with a certain climate and plants and animals adapted to that climate is called a
    Ⓐ home.
    Ⓑ country.
    Ⓒ biome.
    Ⓓ zone.

2. What is precipitation?
    Ⓐ ocean water
    Ⓑ water from plants
    Ⓒ frozen soil
    Ⓓ rain or snow

3. Which best describes the tundra?
    Ⓐ warm, wet biome
    Ⓑ very cold, dry biome
    Ⓒ aquatic biome
    Ⓓ biome with many trees

4. Most of the trees found on the taiga are
    Ⓐ fallen trees.
    Ⓑ palm trees.
    Ⓒ deciduous trees.
    Ⓓ evergreen trees.

5. How many inches of rain fall on a desert in a year?
    Ⓐ fewer than 10 inches
    Ⓑ 20 inches
    Ⓒ 30 inches or more
    Ⓓ more than 40 inches

6. One reason that grassland biomes are important to people is because
    Ⓐ people use wood from their many forests.
    Ⓑ they provide a home for polar bears.
    Ⓒ much of it has been turned into farmland.
    Ⓓ their many trees give people fruits and nuts.

7. What is the name for trees that lose their leaves in autumn?
    Ⓐ spruce trees
    Ⓑ deciduous trees
    Ⓒ evergreen trees
    Ⓓ taiga trees

8. The top part of the rain forest is known as the
    Ⓐ canopy.
    Ⓑ leaves.
    Ⓒ shelter.
    Ⓓ fruit.

9. Saltwater biomes are also called
    Ⓐ taigas.
    Ⓑ freshwater biomes.
    Ⓒ marine biomes.
    Ⓓ lakes, rivers, and streams.

10. Which of these are the tiny, floating plants and animals of marine biomes?
    Ⓐ lily pads
    Ⓑ plankton
    Ⓒ seaweeds
    Ⓓ ocean grasses

Earth's Resources

Natural resources are living and nonliving things found on Earth that help people meet their needs. For instance, oil is a resource found deep under the surface of Earth. As the photograph shows, a pump brings oil to the surface. The fire at the top of the smokestack shows that this well also produces natural gas. Until recently, people did not value this gas, so it was burned as a waste product. Now, well owners often keep the gas to turn it into a very clean source of energy. In this chapter you will learn more about Earth's resources.

What is it?

- It is a solid.
- It forms naturally under the surface of Earth.
- Small bits of it are scattered through soil.

What Are Resources?

Natural resources are living and nonliving things found on Earth that help people meet their needs. These living and nonliving things give us food to eat, clothing to wear, and shelter to protect us from the weather. Some natural resources offer people natural beauty to enjoy and places to relax and play.

Some living things, such as plants and animals, are **renewable resources**. Plants and animals provide us with food. Fruits and vegetables come from plants. Meat and milk come from animals. They also give us materials for making clothes. Cotton for jeans comes from a plant. Wool for sweaters comes from sheep. Leather for shoes comes from cows. Trees provide wood for building houses. When wood is burned, it gives off energy that people can use to stay warm.

Renewable resources can never be used up if they are used properly and not wasted. Besides plants and animals, renewable resources include the soil we use for growing things, the air we breathe, and the water we use for drinking and keeping clean. They also include sources of energy, such as sunlight, the wind, and heat from deep inside Earth.

Some natural resources are nonliving things, such as gas, coal, and oil, which provide energy. These and anything made from them, like plastics, are **nonrenewable resources**. Nonrenewable resources must be used very carefully, because once they are gone, they cannot be replaced. Iron and gold are resources that are taken out of the ground—so are things like gas, coal, and oil. Nonrenewable resources do not grow or change. They are only present on Earth in certain amounts. If they are used up, they are gone.

Renewable and Nonrenewable Resources	
Renewable Resources	**Nonrenewable Resources**
Plants	Iron
Animals	Gold
Soil	Silver
Air	Oil
Water	Coal
Sunlight	Natural Gas
Wind	Plastics

The solar panels on the roof trap the sun's energy to supply heat for this house. Sunlight is a renewable resource because the sun rises every day.

A.
Write the missing word or words in each sentence.

1. Natural resources provide people with _____, clothing, and shelter.

   (plants, food, animals)

2. Plants and animals are both _____ resources.

   (renewable, nonrenewable, nonliving)

3. Iron and oil are both _____ resources.

   (renewable, nonrenewable, living)

4. Renewable resources are resources that can be

   _____.

   (used up, replaced, eaten)

5. Nonrenewable resources are resources that do not

   _____ or change.

   (end, grow, move)

B.
Write R on the line if the natural resource is renewable. Write N on the line if the natural resource is nonrenewable.

_____ 1. tree

_____ 2. oil

_____ 3. water

_____ 4. coal

_____ 5. chicken

C.
Write one or more sentences to answer the question.

Why must people be careful in using natural resources?

_____

_____

_____

_____

How Do We Use Soil?

Soil is the top layer of Earth's surface. It is made of tiny pieces of rocks mixed with natural waste, such as dead leaves. Soil that is rich in natural waste is good for growing food. It is filled with nutrients, or special matter, that plants need to grow. Sometimes, farmers and gardeners add **fertilizer**, or special nutrients, to their soil to make it richer for plants.

All the fruits and vegetables we eat are grown in rich soil. Trees grow in soil, too. We get lumber to build houses and other buildings from trees. When soil is used properly, it stays rich and healthy. When soil is not cared for properly, it loses its richness and its usefulness to plants.

There are many ways that soil can be damaged or **polluted**. Bad farming habits and careless handling of garbage can harm the soil. **Mining**, or taking metals from the ground, can kill plants and harm the soil. Sometimes, soil is completely lost to **erosion**. Erosion happens when rain and wind carry away the richest top layers of soil. Mining, cutting down trees, and building projects can leave the soil unprotected. This makes it easier for erosion to carry away the soil.

People can protect the soil in several ways. Farmers and gardeners can add natural waste to their soil to keep it healthy. Leaves, grass clippings, and animal manure, or waste, can be turned into **compost**. Compost is natural waste that has decayed, or broken down, into soil filled with nutrients. Farmers can plant **windbreaks**, or rows of trees that help block erosion. They can grow special crops to improve soil.

People can protect soil from pollution, such as garbage. They can control mining and building that remove or cover soil. People, plants, and animals need soil. People can work to care for it.

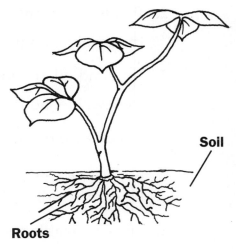

Soil

Roots

Plants use their roots to take the nutrients they need to grow from healthy soil.

A.

Write <u>True</u> if the sentence is true. Write <u>False</u> if the sentence is false.

_____ 1. Soil is the top layer of Earth's surface.

_____ 2. Soil that contains a lot of natural waste is not good for growing plants.

_____ 3. Trees do not grow in soil.

_____ 4. Healthy soil is rich with nutrients.

_____ 5. Erosion happens when soil is carried away by rain and wind.

B.

Write the missing word or words in each sentence.

1. Soil that is rich in _____ is good for growing plants.

   (erosion, natural waste, metal)

2. Farmers can add special nutrients called _____ to soil to make it richer for plants.

   (fertilizer, metals, windbreaks)

3. We get the _____ we use for building houses from trees.

   (lumber, food, compost)

4. Bad farming habits, _____, and careless handling of garbage can all harm the soil.

   (mining, hunting, fishing)

5. Soil that is unprotected is more likely to be washed away by

   _____ .

   (mining, farming, erosion)

C.

Write one or more sentences to answer the question.

How might garbage dumps harm the soil?

_____

_____

_____

_____

How Do We Use Minerals?

Metals and shiny stones that are found under the ground are called **minerals**. Minerals are nonliving materials that form naturally beneath Earth's surface. Some minerals, like gold and silver, are very valuable. Others, like iron, are helpful in building many of the things we use every day. Minerals are important natural resources.

Most of solid Earth is made of minerals. Usually, small bits of minerals are scattered throughout the soil, or are found in pieces of rock. Sometimes, though, a layer of rock contains a large amount of a certain mineral such as iron. The rock that contains the mineral is called an **ore**. When a large supply of ore of an important mineral is found, people mine the land to remove the ore from the ground.

Some minerals are important because of the ways we use them. For example, we use iron to make steel. Steel is used to make cars, to build tall buildings, and for many other things. Glass is made from sand, another mineral. Aluminum is a metal that we use to make things such as soda cans, cooking foil, and airplane parts.

Other minerals are important because they are rare and beautiful. Many of these kinds of minerals, such as gold, silver, and diamonds, are used to make jewelry and objects of art.

Minerals are nonrenewable resources. Once they are removed from the ground, they cannot grow back. But some minerals can be recycled and used over and over again. Metal and glass are two examples of things made from minerals that can be recycled. If people reuse or recycle nonrenewable resources, such as metal, these resources will last longer.

This photo shows a process called strip mining. Any soil and rock covering the ore is stripped off. Then the ore is removed. Miners must return the land to its original condition after the ore is removed.

A. Write the word that best completes each sentence.

glass   nonrenewable   recycle

minerals   ore   remove

1. Metals and shiny stones found under the ground are called

   _____.

2. Rock that contains a large amount of a mineral is called an

   _____.

3. When people mine the land, they _____ the ore from the ground.

4. Minerals are _____ resources.

5. People can _____ some minerals to make them last longer.

6. Two examples of things made from minerals that can be recycled are metal

   and _____.

B. Draw a line to match each mineral to its use.

1. diamonds   used to make cooking foil

2. iron   used to make jewelry

3. sand   used to make steel

4. aluminum   used to make glass

C. Write one or more sentences to answer the question.

Why do you think gold costs more per ounce than silver?

_____

_____

_____

_____

4 How Do We Use Fossil Fuels?

Most of the energy we use every day comes from **fossil fuels**. Fossil fuels form beneath the ground from dead plants and animals that do not break down completely. **Petroleum**, **natural gas**, and **coal** are fossil fuels. Fossil fuels form in different ways, but they are also alike. We can use a tree as an example of how fossil fuels form.

When a tree dies, it falls to the forest floor. In time, the tree will **decompose**, or break down, into very small pieces that form soil and become nutrients for other living things. Sometimes, however, a tree falls to the ground and is buried quickly by layers of soil. Trapped beneath the soil, the tree does not decompose completely. Over time, the pieces of the dead tree can become a fossil fuel.

Petroleum, or crude oil, is a sticky, liquid fossil fuel. Pieces of dead plants and animals settle to the bottoms of lakes and oceans. The dead matter is buried by soil. Each new layer of soil presses on the layers beneath it, trapping the plant and animal pieces. Over millions of years, heat and pressure turn the dead material into petroleum. If temperatures reach a certain point, some of the petroleum changes to **natural gas** that often floats above the liquid.

Coal is a fossil fuel made from dead plants that are buried before they decompose completely. Pressure from the soil presses the dead material tightly, squeezing out water, and leaving a solid fuel.

Petroleum is removed from the ground and changed into products, such as gasoline and kerosene. Pipes carry natural gas to heat homes and buildings. Coal is taken from the ground and shipped to power plants, homes, and factories. Fossil fuels are nonrenewable resources. They give us energy, but they also can pollute land, water, and air.

Petroleum is used to make a variety of products besides fuels.

A. Write the missing word or words in each sentence.

1. Most of the energy we use comes from _____.
   (the wind, fossil fuels, trees)

2. Fossil fuels form over millions of years from dead plants and
   _____.
   (rocks, minerals, animals)

3. Petroleum is also called _____.
   (kerosene, crude oil, gasoline)

4. The sticky, liquid fossil fuel is called _____.
   (fuel oil, kerosene, petroleum)

5. The fossil fuel that forms when petroleum reaches a certain temperature is
   _____.
   (gasoline, natural gas, air)

6. The solid fossil fuel made from dead plants is _____.
   (coal, plastic, petroleum)

B. Put a ✔ next to the ways we use fossil fuels.

_____ 1. Petroleum is used to make gasoline.

_____ 2. Petroleum is used to make coal.

_____ 3. Natural gas is used to heat homes.

_____ 4. Natural gas is used to make gasoline.

_____ 5. Coal is used to make electricity.

C. Write one or more sentences to answer the question.

What can people do to make fossil fuel supplies last longer?

_____

_____

_____

_____

LESSON 5

How Do We Use Air?

The air around us is one of our most important natural resources. It is made of a special mixture of gases, such as **oxygen** and **nitrogen**, that make life possible for humans and other living things. Without air, nothing on Earth could live.

Air forms the **atmosphere**. The atmosphere is like an envelope of air that surrounds Earth. It is held close to Earth by Earth's **gravity**. If there were no gravity, Earth's atmosphere would float off into space. Earth's atmosphere contains 78 percent nitrogen and 21 percent oxygen. The remaining one percent is made of **carbon dioxide** and other gases. The atmosphere also holds dust particles and water droplets.

Both plants and animals need air to live, but they use it in different ways. Animals take in oxygen when they breathe in, and give off carbon dioxide when they breathe out. Plants, on the other hand, take in carbon dioxide and give off oxygen through tiny holes in their leaves. Much of the oxygen in the atmosphere comes from plants. This explains why trees and other plants are so important for humans and other animals. Plants help give us the oxygen we need to breathe and stay alive. At the same time, we help give plants the carbon dioxide they need.

All living things need clean air. But many things people do can pollute the air and make it unhealthy for breathing. Cars, factories, fires, and power plants all produce waste materials, such as harmful gases and tiny solids, that escape into the atmosphere. By driving less, using less electricity, and being careful about what we burn, we can help make sure our air will be cleaner and safe to breathe. We also can keep the air healthy by protecting and planting trees and plants around the world.

The Oxygen–Carbon Dioxide Cycle

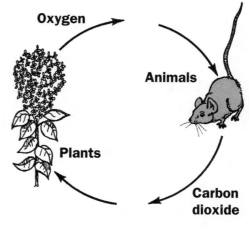

Oxygen

Animals

Plants

Carbon dioxide

Plants take in carbon dioxide from the atmosphere and release oxygen. Animals take in oxygen from the atmosphere and release carbon dioxide.

A.

Underline the correct word or words in each sentence.

83

1. Air is a mixture of (oxygen, nitrogen, gases).

2. The atmosphere is an envelope of (air, pollution, gravity) that surrounds Earth.

3. The atmosphere is held close to Earth by Earth's (gravity, air, gases).

4. Both plants and animals need (oxygen, carbon dioxide, air) to survive.

5. Much of the oxygen in the atmosphere comes from (plants, animals, factories).

6. Cars put (oxygen, harmful gases, nitrogen) into the atmosphere.

7. We can help keep the air healthy by (planting trees, building factories, producing gases) around the world.

B.

Write <u>Healthy</u> or <u>Unhealthy</u> to show if the words describe something that is good or something that is bad for the atmosphere.

_____ 1. burn more trash

_____ 2. plant more trees

_____ 3. drive less

_____ 4. use more electricity

_____ 5. cut down more forests

C.

Write one or more sentences to answer the question.

Why do many people like to grow plants in their homes?

_____

_____

_____

_____

_____

_____

How Do We Use Water?

Sometimes Earth is called the blue planet. Water covers almost three fourths of Earth. Most of that water is ocean **saltwater**. The ocean's waters are too salty for drinking and for watering our crops. While oceans are important, they do not give us the freshwater that living things need to live.

Like soil and air, freshwater is one of Earth's important natural resources. Living things depend on water. They are also made of water. The human body, for example, is almost two-thirds water. It is good, then, that water is a renewable resource. But, as you already know, renewable resources need care.

Only three percent of Earth's water is freshwater. Most of that water is frozen in the polar ice caps and in glaciers. All life depends on less than one percent of Earth's water supply. Let's say that another way. Imagine all the water on Earth filled 26 large milk jugs. All of Earth's freshwater would fill less than one of those jugs. And all of the freshwater that we can use wouldn't fill a teaspoon.

People use water in many ways. We drink it. We use it to keep clean and to wash dishes, clothes, and other things. We use flowing water to make electricity. And we enjoy swimming and boating.

Water is a precious natural resource we cannot waste or pollute. We waste water when we take long showers, flush toilets too often, or let water run when we are not using it. We pollute water when we pour harmful materials down kitchen and bathroom sinks. We pollute water when we throw wastes into water and bury wastes in the ground. When we pollute water, we harm the drinking water for all living things. If we want water to be clean and safe, we must save and protect it.

The flowing water in the stream supplies power to turn the waterwheel.

Like the waterwheel in the picture above, this dam uses the power of flowing water. It produces electricity for thousands of homes and businesses.

A. Write <u>True</u> if the sentence is true. Write <u>False</u> if the sentence is false.

_____ 1. Water is a renewable resource.

_____ 2. Saltwater is good for drinking.

_____ 3. Water covers more than three fourths of Earth's surface.

_____ 4. Human beings are made of about one-third water.

_____ 5. More than half of Earth's water is freshwater.

B. Write the missing word or words in each sentence.

1. Most of Earth's water is in the _____.
   (oceans, atmosphere, ground)

2. We use flowing water to make _____.
   (salt, electricity, resources)

3. People waste water by _____.
   (swimming, boating, taking long showers)

4. People pollute water when they add _____ to
   the water.
   (dust particles, harmful materials, too many fish)

5. People can help prevent water pollution by not pouring

   _____ down kitchen sinks.
   (dirty water, boiling water, anything harmful)

C. Write one or more sentences to answer the question.

How can you save water when you are getting ready for school in the morning?

_____

_____

_____

_____

_____

Recycle Paper

You need:

- **newspapers**
- **large bowl**
- **water**
- **stirring stick**
- **safety goggles**

- **warm water**
- **small bowl**
- **laundry starch**
- **screen**

- **teaspoon**
- **flat pan**
- **plastic wrap**
- **large books**

In this activity you will make paper.

Follow these steps:

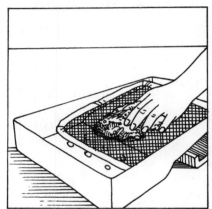

1. Tear two sheets of newspaper into small pieces. Place the pieces in the large bowl with water. Mix the paper and water into mush.

2. Put on your safety goggles. Fill the small bowl with warm water. Add two teaspoons of laundry starch and stir. Pour the mixture over the newspaper mush and stir.

3. Place the screen in the pan. Use your hands to take some newspaper mush from the bowl and spread it on the screen.

4. Place the screen on a stack of newspapers. Cover the newspaper mush with plastic wrap. Place several large books on top of it. Then, remove the books and plastic wrap. Let the paper dry.

Write answers to these questions.

1. How is your paper like newspaper or writing paper? How is it different?

_____

2. Why might someone want to build a factory that makes paper from old paper rather than from trees?

_____

Darken the circle next to the correct answer.

1. What are three renewable resources?
    Ⓐ plants, sunlight, animals
    Ⓑ water, oil, air
    Ⓒ plants, wind, coal
    Ⓓ gas, coal, oil

2. What are three nonrenewable resources?
    Ⓐ plants, sunlight, animals
    Ⓑ water, oil, air
    Ⓒ plants, wind, coal
    Ⓓ gas, coal, oil

3. The top layer of Earth's surface is
    Ⓐ compost.
    Ⓑ ore.
    Ⓒ soil.
    Ⓓ metals.

4. Soil is made of rocks, metals, and
    Ⓐ animals.
    Ⓑ natural waste.
    Ⓒ crude oil.
    Ⓓ plants.

5. What are the nonliving materials that form naturally beneath Earth's surface?
    Ⓐ minerals
    Ⓑ renewable resources
    Ⓒ plastics
    Ⓓ glass

6. A layer of rock that contains a large amount of a certain mineral is
    Ⓐ a fossil fuel.
    Ⓑ an ore.
    Ⓒ a renewable resource.
    Ⓓ a mine.

7. Most of the energy we use every day comes from
    Ⓐ burning wood.
    Ⓑ water.
    Ⓒ fossil fuels.
    Ⓓ the sun.

8. What are three important fossil fuels?
    Ⓐ wood, coal, petroleum
    Ⓑ wind, water, the sun
    Ⓒ petroleum, wood, the sun
    Ⓓ coal, petroleum, natural gas

9. The envelope of air surrounding Earth is called the
    Ⓐ gravity.
    Ⓑ nitrogen.
    Ⓒ atmosphere.
    Ⓓ oxygen.

10. What covers more than 70 percent of Earth's surface?
    Ⓐ ore
    Ⓑ water
    Ⓒ lakes and rivers
    Ⓓ soil

CHAPTER

6

Weather

The atmosphere—the envelope of air that surrounds Earth—is the source of Earth's weather. Weather conditions change from one place to another. Some areas are very windy, and others are not. Hurricanes sometimes form over the oceans. Tornadoes, like the one shown in this photograph, form mainly over land. In fact, there are more tornadoes in the United States than anywhere else on Earth. In this chapter you will learn about the atmosphere and the forces that give us weather.

What is it?

- It forms where two air masses meet.
- Its name comes from its temperature.
- It can cause changes in the weather.

What Are the Layers in the Atmosphere?

You have learned that the envelope of air surrounding Earth is called the atmosphere. Scientists have found that there are five different layers in the atmosphere. These layers are the **troposphere**, the **stratosphere**, the **mesosphere**, the **thermosphere**, and the **exosphere**. Scientists can tell one layer from another by differences in temperature in the layers.

The troposphere is the layer of air closest to Earth's surface. The air in the troposphere is warmer at the bottom and gets cooler at higher **altitudes**, or higher up from Earth's surface. The troposphere contains about 75 percent of all the air in the atmosphere and most of the moisture. All of Earth's weather happens in the troposphere.

Above the troposphere is the stratosphere. The air in the stratosphere is colder at lower altitudes and becomes warmer at higher altitudes. The stratosphere contains Earth's **ozone** layer. Ozone protects us from the sun's harmful rays.

Above the stratosphere is the mesosphere. Here again, the air continues to cool at higher altitudes. Huge windstorms occur in the mesosphere, but they are so high above Earth's surface that we don't feel them.

Above the mesosphere is the thermosphere. Temperatures in the thermosphere increase from the bottom to the top. The top of the thermosphere receives the most energy from the sun. Temperatures at the outer edge of the thermosphere can reach extremely high temperatures.

Above the thermosphere is the exosphere. The exosphere is made mostly of the light gases helium and hydrogen. Beyond this final layer of Earth's atmosphere is the emptiness of outer space.

The Layers of Earth's Atmosphere

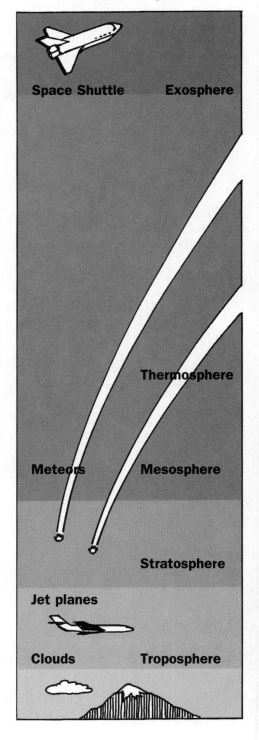

Space Shuttle   Exosphere

Thermosphere

Meteors   Mesosphere

Stratosphere

Jet planes

Clouds   Troposphere

A. Write the word or words that best complete each sentence.

1. The envelope of air that surrounds Earth is called the

   _____.

   (atmosphere, stratosphere, mesosphere)

2. The layer of the atmosphere closest to the ground is called the

   _____.

   (stratosphere, mesosphere, troposphere)

3. In the thermosphere, the air in higher altitudes is

   _____ air in lower altitudes.

   (cooler than, warmer than, the same as)

4. The highest layer of the atmosphere is called the

   _____.

   (mesosphere, troposphere, exosphere)

5. Earth's weather happens in the _____.
   (troposphere, stratosphere, exosphere)

B. Write <u>True</u> if the sentence is true. Write <u>False</u> if the sentence is false.

_____ 1. The air in the troposphere is warm at the bottom, but becomes cooler at higher altitudes.

_____ 2. The troposphere contains very little moisture.

_____ 3. In the stratosphere the air is warmer at higher altitudes.

_____ 4. Earth's ozone layer protects us from harmful sun rays.

_____ 5. The lower part of the thermosphere receives the most energy from the sun.

C. Write one or more sentences to answer the question.

Which layer of the atmosphere do you think affects human beings the most? Explain.

_____

_____

LESSON 2

How Do Clouds and Rain Form?

Why do clouds form? Why do puddles disappear? The answers can be found in the **water cycle**, or the way water changes and moves in Earth's atmosphere and on land. Heat from the sun, or **solar energy**, together with Earth's gravity, keep the water cycle moving.

The water cycle has three important steps. Heat energy from the sun makes water **molecules**, or the smallest particles of water, in the oceans, lakes, rivers, streams, and even puddles, move faster. When a liquid water molecule gains enough heat energy, it changes to a gas called **water vapor**. This change from a liquid to a gas is called **evaporation**. The amount of water vapor in the air is called **humidity**. When air holds large amounts of water vapor, the air has high humidity. You can feel air with high humidity. The air feels damp on your skin.

In the second step, water vapor moves away from the surface of Earth and rises into the atmosphere. As air moves higher through the troposphere, it cools. As water vapor cools, it changes to a liquid. This change is called **condensation**. But condensation happens only with help from tiny particles, such as dust or sea salt, in the air. They give liquid water a surface on which to form. When many particles form, you see fog, icy frosts, and clouds.

Clouds appear and move through the sky. When the water droplets in clouds become large, they also become heavy. In the third step of the water cycle, gravity pulls these heavy drops toward Earth as rain, snow, hail, or sleet. Precipitation falls into oceans, lakes, and rivers. Some sinks deep within Earth, forming **groundwater**. Rains flow along the surface, forming **runoff**. In time, all of this water returns to the oceans where the water cycle begins again.

The Water Cycle

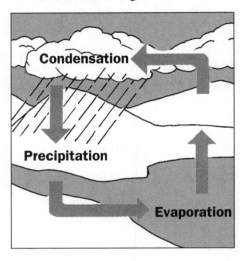

A.

Underline the correct word or words in each sentence.

1. Heat from the sun causes (molecules, droplets, runoff) of water on the ground to move faster.

2. When there is a lot of water vapor in the air, the humidity is (high, heavy, low).

3. In the water cycle, water on Earth's surface moves into the air by changing into (water vapor, rain, snow).

4. Clouds are made of droplets of (water vapor, minerals, liquid water) floating high in the air.

5. Water that flows over Earth's surface is called (groundwater, runoff, precipitation).

B.

Draw lines to match each word with its definition.

1. evaporation   water that falls from clouds

2. humidity   water beneath Earth's surface

3. condensation   the change from liquid water to water vapor

4. precipitation   the change from water vapor to liquid water

5. groundwater   the amount of water vapor in the air

C.

Write one or more sentences to answer the question.

Does the water cycle have a beginning and an end? Explain.

_____

_____

_____

_____

_____

_____

LESSON 3

What Is Air Pressure?

Do you remember a time when you rode your bike so fast that you could feel the air pushing against your skin and bicycle? You pushed back, pressing harder on the pedals. Like all matter, air has weight, and that weight pushes against you all the time. Why doesn't the air crush you? The answer is in your body. Your body holds air also. That air pushes against the air around you with an equal force. **Meteorologists**, or people who study weather, call this force **air pressure**.

Air pressure is not the same everywhere on Earth's surface. For example, the place where the air meets the ocean is called **sea level**. The air presses down at sea level with an average force of 14.7 pounds per square inch. But as you move above sea level, the air changes. Air **expands**, or spreads out. When air expands, there is more space between each air molecule. The air has less weight or force. Air pressure on top of Earth's tallest mountains is less than air pressure at sea level.

Temperature changes air pressure. Molecules of warm air move faster than molecules of cool air. When they move faster, they spread apart and lift into the atmosphere. As they lift, there is less pressure on Earth's surface. When air cools, however, the molecules move more slowly and are closer together. Cool air has higher air pressure, or is heavier, than warm air. Cool air sinks and moves to fill the spaces left as warm air rises.

Meteorologists measure temperature with **thermometers**. Thermometers measure temperature in degrees Fahrenheit (°F) or degrees Celsius (°C). Meteorologists use **barometers** to measure air pressure. Changes in air temperature cause changes in air pressure. Meteorologists know that changes in air pressure often bring changes in weather.

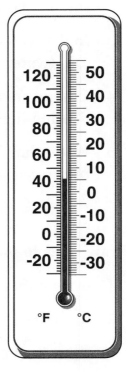

This thermometer has a double scale—one for degrees Fahrenheit (°F) and one for degrees Celsius (°C). Notice that 32°F equals 0°C. What does 20°C equal?

Cool air is more dense, so it sinks. As it sinks, the cool air pushes warm air up, causing warm air to rise.

94

A. Write the missing word or words in each sentence.

1. The weight, or force, of the air in the atmosphere is called

   _____.

   (air pressure, temperature, weather)

2. The average weight of Earth's atmosphere at sea level is about

   14.7 _____ per square inch.

   (tons, ounces, pounds)

3. Changes in _____ cause changes in air pressure.

   (temperature, movement, flow rate)

4. Heavier, cooler air flows _____ spaces left by

   lighter, warmer air.

   (into, away from, around)

5. Fahrenheit and Celsius are two scales for measuring

   _____.

   (air pressure, temperature, air movement)

6. Barometers are used to measure _____.

   (air pressure, temperature, air movement)

B. Draw a line to complete each sentence.

1. Meteorologists   are used to measure temperature.

2. Air pressure   is the weight of air pressing on Earth.

3. Thermometers   are people who study the weather.

4. Fahrenheit   is one scale for measuring temperature.

C. Write one or more sentences to answer the question.

The weather has been sunny and cool for the last three days. What would you expect the air pressure to be? Explain.

_____

_____

4 What Makes the Wind Blow?

How are a gentle breeze and air that turns your umbrella inside out alike? They are both examples of **wind**. Wind happens when air moves from places where there is high pressure to places where there is low pressure. The larger the difference in pressures between these two places, the stronger the winds are.

How do these different air pressures happen? Remember that the sun heats Earth, and that changes in temperature cause changes in air pressure. As air warms, it expands and rises, losing air pressure. As air cools, it **contracts**, or moves closer together. Cool air is heavy and thick and has high pressure.

To understand winds and weather better, you also need to know about **air masses**. An air mass is a huge body of air that forms above a large area of land or water. The land or water beneath the air mass gives the air certain properties, such as its temperature and humidity. For example, an air mass that forms above Greenland is very cold and has very little water vapor, or low humidity. Air masses form above other parts of Earth, too. They are named for their properties. Warm air masses are called **tropical**. Cold air masses are called **polar**, unless they form over very cold areas. Then, they are called **arctic** air masses. If the air mass has low humidity, it is called a **continental** air mass. And if the air mass holds a lot of water vapor, or has high humidity, it is a **maritime** air mass. Air masses are always moving and changing, giving us winds and other weather.

Meteorologists use **anemometers** to measure the speed of wind. A **weather vane** measures the direction of wind, or the place from which the wind blows. A south wind, for example, blows from the south. Changes in wind speed and direction help meteorologists understand changes in the weather.

The anemometer on the top of this machine turns to measure wind speed. The arrow beneath the anemometer is a weather vane. It points to show the direction of wind.

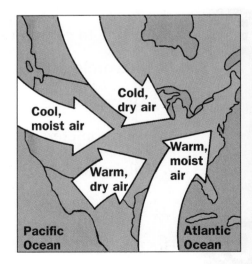

The warm, moist air mass coming into the United States from the Gulf of Mexico is called a maritime tropical air mass. What is the cold, dry air mass coming into the United States from Canada called?

A. Write <u>True</u> if the sentence is true. Write <u>False</u> if the sentence is false.

_____ 1. The movement of air is called wind.

_____ 2. Warm air rises and has low pressure.

_____ 3. Cool air expands and has high pressure.

_____ 4. Cold air masses are called polar air masses.

_____ 5. Weather vanes measure the speed of the wind.

B. Write the word or words that best complete each sentence.

air mass	maritime	winds
continental	tropical	

1. When air travels from one pressure area to another, _____ happen.

2. A huge body of air with certain properties, such as temperature and humidity, is a(n) _____.

3. Warm air masses are called _____ air masses.

4. Air masses with low humidity are called _____ air masses.

5. Air masses with high humidity are called _____ air masses.

C. Write one or more sentences to answer the question.

The word *maritime* means "of the sea." Why do you think air masses with high humidity are called maritime air masses?

_____

_____

_____

_____

What Are Fronts?

Meteorologists study the movement of air masses closely. They know that when air masses move, weather changes. They also know that moving air masses follow certain rules. This makes it possible for meteorologists to **forecast**, or tell what will or may happen, with the weather.

Air masses with different properties, such as temperature and humidity, don't mix easily. When two air masses with different properties meet, they form a zone called a **front**. A front stretches up, in, and across the air mass it meets. Fronts are described by their temperatures. A **cold front**, for example, is cooler than a **warm front**.

When a cold air mass approaches a warm air mass, meteorologists watch carefully. Cold fronts often bring large changes in weather. Remember that cold air is heavy. It moves beneath the warm air mass, forcing the warm air to rise. If the warm air holds lots of moisture, powerful thunderstorms can form as the warm air is pushed up. When the storms lose their strength, cooler temperatures remain.

When a warm air mass approaches a cold air mass, the results are different. Because the cold air is heavier than the warm air, the cold air stays close to the ground. The lighter, warm air is pushed up, but the warm front is gentle and not as large as the cold front. Changes in the weather are usually less powerful. The rising warm air cools, and may produce light, steady precipitation.

Sometimes, two air masses meet and neither moves. When both air masses remain still, a **stationary front** forms. Clouds appear. Steady drizzles, or gentle showers of rain, may fall for days. This mild weather may stay until changes in the atmosphere cause one of the air masses to move.

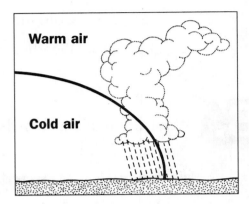

In a cold front, the cold air mass pushes under the warm air mass, forcing the warm air to rise quickly and causing heavy storms.

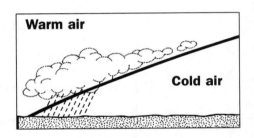

In a warm front, the warm air mass pushes over the cold air mass, but the warm air rises slowly, causing light, steady precipitation.

A. Underline the correct word in each sentence.

1. The zone where a warm air mass and a cold air mass meet is called a (front, wind, cloud).

2. Meteorologists (delay, forecast, control) the weather and tell how it will or may change.

3. In a cold front, the cold air mass moves (alongside, over, beneath) the warm air mass.

4. In a warm front, the warm air mass moves (alongside, over, under) the cold air mass.

5. A front that is not moving or is moving very slowly is a (cold, warm, stationary) front.

B. Draw lines to match each weather condition on the left with a weather change on the right.

1. cold front moves in   weather becomes stormy

2. warm front moves in   weather turns cooler

3. stationary front forms   light, steady precipitation starts

4. cold front passes by   long period of mild weather

C. Write one or more sentences to answer the question.

Meteorologists use weather satellites to collect information about the atmosphere. How do you think weather satellites have helped scientists?

_____

_____

_____

_____

_____

How Do People Forecast Weather?

As you know, meteorologists study the weather. They collect information and search for patterns that help them forecast weather. It's important for people to know what kinds of weather to expect. Then they can know what clothes to wear and if roads are safe to drive. They can know when a dangerous storm, such as a **hurricane**, forms over the ocean. Or they can know if the weather is likely to produce another dangerous and powerful land storm, called a **tornado**.

To understand the weather, meteorologists must collect a lot of weather data, or information. They depend on special tools, such as anemometers, thermometers, barometers, weather vanes, and tools that measure humidity. Special balloons carry tools into the upper parts of the atmosphere. Information from the balloons is sent back to meteorologists working on the ground. Today, meteorologists also use **satellites**, **radar**, and computers to collect and study data. Meteorologists use **weather stations** to hold their equipment.

Weather **satellites** collect information from above Earth's atmosphere and send it back to Earth. The pictures of moving clouds and storms you see on television are sent from these special satellites.

Radar tracks the movement and speed of storms from Earth. Radar sends radio waves into the atmosphere. These waves bounce off raindrops, ice particles, and clouds and return to Earth. Meteorologists record the time that passes between the time the waves are sent and the time they return.

Once meteorologists have collected and studied data from all of these sources, they create weather maps that use special symbols, or marks. By studying these maps closely, meteorologists can search for patterns that help them forecast the weather.

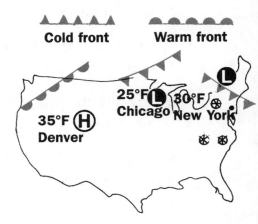

Meteorologists use maps like this to show fronts, temperatures, and other weather conditions. What do you think **H** and **L** stand for?

A. Write the missing word or words in each sentence.

1. To understand the weather, meteorologists collect a lot of weather

   _____.

   (data, symbols, stories)

2. Weather stations are full of _____ meteorologists use to study weather.

   (satellites, fronts, equipment)

3. The pictures of clouds that you see on television weather reports come from _____.

   (balloons, radio stations, satellites)

4. Radar uses _____ to collect weather information.

   (cameras, radio waves, symbols)

5. Meteorologists use special _____ to show weather data on weather maps.

   (symbols, fronts, radar)

B. Write <u>True</u> if the sentence is true. Write <u>False</u> if the sentence is false.

_____ 1. Weather stations circle high above Earth.

_____ 2. Radar uses television pictures.

_____ 3. Weather stations contain tools, such as thermometers, barometers, anemometers, and weather vanes.

_____ 4. Weather maps are used to predict the weather.

C. Write one or more sentences to answer the questions.

Have you ever used weather forecasts from the radio, television, or newspaper? If so, for what purpose? If not, for what purpose do you think you might use them in the future?

_____

_____

_____

CHAPTER 6

Make a Wind Speed Indicator

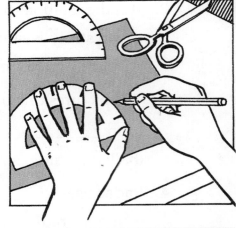

You need:

- **protractor**
- **paper**
- **pencil**
- **scissors**
- **centimeter ruler**
- **string**
- **stapler**
- **tape**
- **foam ball**

In this activity you will measure wind speed.

Follow these steps:

1. Place the protractor on the paper. Trace around it. Mark the paper protractor at regular intervals.

2. Cut out the paper protractor. Then, cut a section of string about 20 cm long.

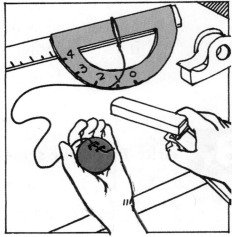

3. Tape the paper protractor to the real protractor. Then, tape the protractor to the ruler.

4. Staple and tape one end of the string to the foam ball. Tape the other end to the center of the straight edge of the protractor.

5. Go outside. Hold your wind speed indicator by the ruler. Point the other end of the ruler directly into the wind. Read the wind speed every minute for five minutes. Write the speed down.

Write answers to these questions.

1. What was the lowest wind speed you recorded? The highest?

2. Is this weather normal for your area? Why or why not?

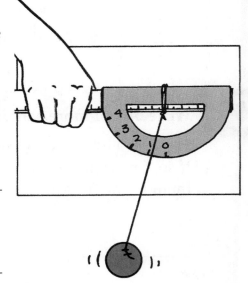

Darken the circle next to the correct answer.

1. The layer of Earth's atmosphere nearest Earth is the
   Ⓐ troposphere.
   Ⓑ stratosphere.
   Ⓒ mesosphere.
   Ⓓ thermosphere.

2. Changes in the weather happen in the
   Ⓐ troposphere.
   Ⓑ stratosphere.
   Ⓒ mesosphere.
   Ⓓ thermosphere.

3. What describes how much water vapor is in the air?
   Ⓐ evaporation
   Ⓑ humidity
   Ⓒ condensation
   Ⓓ precipitation

4. Precipitation that sinks into the ground is called
   Ⓐ groundwater.
   Ⓑ runoff.
   Ⓒ condensation.
   Ⓓ evaporation.

5. What is the weight of the air in the atmosphere called?
   Ⓐ humidity
   Ⓑ Fahrenheit
   Ⓒ air pressure
   Ⓓ Celsius

6. A huge body of air that forms above a large area is called
   Ⓐ thick air.
   Ⓑ maritime air.
   Ⓒ an air mass.
   Ⓓ an anemometer.

7. Which tool is used to measure the speed of the wind?
   Ⓐ thermometer
   Ⓑ barometer
   Ⓒ weather vane
   Ⓓ anemometer

8. A zone between two air masses that are not moving is a
   Ⓐ barometer.
   Ⓑ cold front.
   Ⓒ warm front.
   Ⓓ stationary front.

9. Which of the following takes pictures of clouds from space?
   Ⓐ satellite
   Ⓑ weather station
   Ⓒ radar
   Ⓓ weather map

10. To forecast the weather, meteorologists need a lot of weather
   Ⓐ fronts.
   Ⓑ data.
   Ⓒ symbols.
   Ⓓ changes.

Careers

Marine Biologist

What scientist studies whales, starfish, and octopuses? A marine biologist studies all the animals and plants in the ocean. These life forms can be very large, like whales, or too small to see with your eyes.

Marine biologists often work on boats or dive underwater to observe ocean plants and animals. They use special cameras underwater. Marine biologists study what helps and harms ocean life. Sometimes they learn things that are useful to people. Some marine biologists have discovered medicines.

Geologist

A geologist studies Earth. Geologists work in many places, including the ocean. Sometimes they drill holes deep into Earth to collect rocks and soil. By studying rocks and soil, geologists learn about Earth's different layers. They study fossils and learn about Earth's history.

Geologists sometimes make discoveries that are useful to people, like water or oil. They can also suggest good places to build roads, buildings, and tunnels.

Soil Conservationist

Plants need soil to grow, but sometimes rain or wind wears soil away. A soil conservationist works with farmers to find ways to protect the soil.

Soil conservationists may suggest crops that help hold soil in place. Soil conservationists can also teach farmers ways to plow fields and plant crops that will keep wind or rain from carrying away the soil.

Unit 3
Physical Science

Energy comes in many forms. The energy that moves this "bullet train" in Japan more than 130 miles per hour comes from magnets. In the background, you can see the volcano called Mt. Fuji. Heat from volcanoes is also a source of energy. The sun shining on the train is another source of energy. You'll learn about many energy sources in this unit.

How Energy Changes

The basketball players bounce the ball up and down the court, circle and weave, then jump toward the basket. The ball bounces back from the rim. The players battle for the ball, then try again. One player bends his knees, and the people watching hold their breath. They know he's getting ready to jump above the rim and dunk the ball. When he scores, fans scream. There are many forms of energy on a basketball court. Can you name some? This chapter will help you answer that question.

What is it?

- It is a kind of energy.
- It is produced when air moves.
- It can move through solids, liquids, and gases, but not empty space.

What Are Temperature and Heat?

In winter the air outdoors can get cold. People wear sweaters and coats to stay warm. In summer the air outdoors gets hot. People wear T-shirts and shorts to stay cool. **Temperature** is a measure of how hot or cold something is. Temperature is measured with a thermometer marked in degrees. The greater the number of degrees, the higher the temperature.

Something that is hot has a high temperature. A cup of hot soup has a high temperature, so does a pot of boiling water. In summer when the weather is hot, the outdoor air has a high temperature.

Something that is cold has a low temperature. A bowl of ice cream has a low temperature, so does a cube of ice. In winter when the weather is cold, the outdoor air has a low temperature.

Heat is energy that moves from one object to another when the two objects have different temperatures. Imagine how cold your hands can get when you've been outdoors on a cold windy day. Now, imagine holding a cup of hot, steaming soup in your cold hands. Heat moves from the cup to your hands, making your hands feel warmer. Heat energy always moves from hot to cold.

All matter is made of tiny particles, or **molecules**. Heat energy makes these tiny particles move. When something is hot, it has more heat energy and its molecules move faster. When something is cold, it has less heat energy and its molecules move more slowly. The molecules in cold water do not move very fast. If a pot of cold water is placed over a hot flame, heat energy moves into the water. The water molecules move faster and faster as the water heats up. If enough heat energy is added to the water, the water will boil.

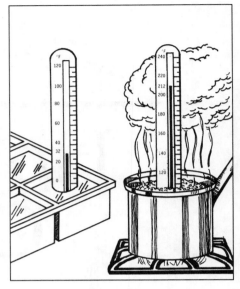

Hot objects have a high temperature. Cold objects have a low temperature.

Heat energy moves from hot objects to cold objects. Heat from the hot pan melts the butter.

A.

Write True if the sentence is true. Write False if the sentence is false.

_____ 1. Temperature is a measure of how hot or cold something is.

_____ 2. The greater the number of degrees measured by a thermometer, the lower the temperature.

_____ 3. Heat energy moves from cold to hot.

_____ 4. Hot objects have more heat energy than cold objects.

_____ 5. The molecules in an object move slower when the object is cold.

B.

Write the words <u>higher temperature</u> or <u>lower temperature</u> to complete each sentence.

1. A temperature of 75°F is a _____ than 50°F.

2. A temperature of 0°C is a _____ than 12°C.

3. Something that is hot has a _____ than something that is cold.

4. A bowl of ice cream has a _____ than a cup of hot soup.

5. A glass of cold lemonade has a _____ than a cup of warm milk.

6. A sunny patch of sidewalk has a _____ than the shady sidewalk under a tree.

C.

Write one or more sentences to answer the question.

What happens to the molecules in butter as butter is taken from the refrigerator and placed in a hot pan?

_____

_____

_____

_____

_____

LESSON 2 How Does Heat Move?

Heat energy can move in three ways. **Conduction** is the flow of heat through the movement of molecules in an object, or from one object to another object that it is touching. Licking an ice cream cone causes the ice cream to melt on your tongue. Heat moves from your tongue to the ice cream by conduction.

Some materials conduct heat better than others. Have you ever put a metal spoon in a cup of hot soup? In a few seconds, the spoon becomes too hot to touch. The heat energy from the hot soup moves through the metal very quickly. Metal is a good conductor. Most cooking pans are made of metal. Heat is easily conducted through the metal. Pans often have wooden or plastic handles that stay cool when the rest of the pan is hot. Wood and plastic do not conduct heat well.

Convection is the circular motion of heat through liquids, such as water, or gases, such as air. The way heat moves through a pan of water on a stove is a good example of convection. The molecules of water at the bottom of the pot, near the flame, heat up and move faster. As they move faster, they spread apart. The water with more space among the molecules is lighter, so it moves up to the top of the pan. Colder water with molecules that are closer together, or more dense, is heavier. It moves down to the bottom of the pan. Then, this colder water heats up and moves toward the top. This circular motion is convection.

In conduction, heat energy moves through objects. In convection, heat energy moves in a circular motion through a liquid or gas. But **radiation** is the movement of heat energy through space. Heat energy from the sun radiates through space to reach Earth. You can feel it on a sunny day. Heat radiates from the flames of a campfire, although there may also be some convection in the air around a campfire.

In conduction, heat moves from the hot soup through the metal of the spoon.

In convection, the hotter water at the bottom of the pot rises to the top. Cooler water at the top sinks to the bottom.

In radiation, the heat from a campfire moves outward into the air.

A. Write <u>conduction</u>, <u>convection</u>, or <u>radiation</u> to complete each sentence.

1. The flow of heat through an object is _____.

2. The flow of heat between two objects that are touching is

   _____.

3. The circular flow of heat energy in a liquid or a gas is

   _____.

4. The movement of heat energy through space is

   _____.

5. The heat that moves out from the flames in a campfire is an example of

   _____.

6. Heat moving along a spoon placed in a hot bowl of soup is an example of

   _____.

B. Label each picture with <u>conduction</u>, <u>convection</u>, or <u>radiation</u> to show how heat moves.

 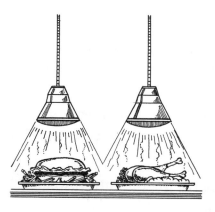 

_____ _____ _____

C. Write one or more sentences to answer the question.

If there is a space heater in a room, how does heat energy move from the heater to heat the room and the objects in the room?

_____

_____

3 What Are Other Forms of Energy?

You have learned that heat is one form of energy. Another form is **light energy**. Light energy, like heat energy, can travel through the emptiness of outer space. Light can also travel through clear materials, such as air, water, and glass. Light from the sun travels through outer space to Earth. Objects that give off light include the sun and other stars, fires, and electric lamps.

Sound energy cannot move through empty space, but it can move through air, water, metal, and other materials. Sound is produced when something makes air molecules vibrate, or move back and forth very rapidly. A ringing bell produces waves of sound in the air around it. The sound waves travel through the air to your ear, and you hear the ringing sound. When people speak, their vocal chords make sound waves that travel through the air.

Mechanical energy is the energy of moving objects. Sound is a type of mechanical energy because it is produced by motion. Water flowing in a river and horses galloping across a field are examples of mechanical energy. You use mechanical energy to chew food, carry books, and run to home plate during a baseball game.

Electrical energy, or electricity, usually flows through metal wires. Electricity is used to run computers, motors, telephones, light bulbs, and many other objects people use every day. Most of the electricity people use is produced in power plants and carried by power lines to homes, office buildings, and factories. Electricity is also produced by batteries, such as those used in flashlights or wrist watches. Lightning is a form of electricity that is not contained in wires. During a storm, a lightning bolt can travel from the clouds to the ground.

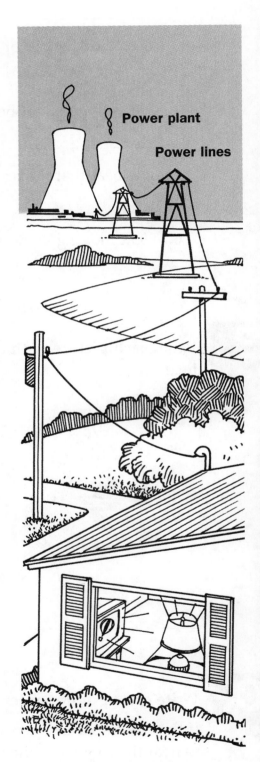

Electricity is produced in power plants and flows through wires to homes.

CHAPTER

8

Simple Machines

This X-ray of a hand shows bones and joints. A hand is part of a simple machine. For instance, pick up a book from your desk. While your elbow stays in place, muscles and bones in your hand and arm work to lift the book. Your elbow works as a fixed point in a lever. Together, your hand, arm, and elbow are a simple machine. This chapter discusses simple machines. As you read, think of other parts of your body that work like simple machines.

What is it?

- It does work with one movement.
- You can use it to move heavy furniture.
- One form of it is used in bottle tops.

When you push a book across your desk, you change the position of the book by moving it to a different place on the desk. The book changes position because you apply a **force** to it. A force is a push or a pull that changes the position of an object. It takes energy to apply a force.

When a baseball player throws a ball across the field, a force is applied to the ball. The force changes the position of the ball. The distance the ball travels depends on the amount of force the player applies to it. If the player throws the ball softly, it will not go very far. If the player throws the ball hard, the ball will travel farther. A strong force causes a large change in the position of an object. A weak force causes a small change in the position of an object.

A force always acts in some direction. The direction could be up or down, backward or forward, or left or right. Someone pushing a grocery cart at the supermarket is applying a forward force to the cart. Someone pulling on a rope in a tug-of-war is applying a backward force to the rope. Someone picking up litter off the street is applying an upward force to the litter.

Gravity is a force that pulls objects toward each other. Earth's gravity applies a force to your body all the time. When you jump up you always come back down. Earth's gravity pulls you toward Earth. Gravity can pull on objects even if they are not touching. Gravity keeps the moon in orbit around Earth. Earth's gravity pulls on the moon, and the moon's gravity pulls on Earth. Gravity also keeps Earth in orbit around the sun. All objects have gravity. Large objects, like Earth and the moon, have strong gravity. Small objects, like people and books, have weak gravity.

A force is a push or pull that changes the position of an object. This baseball player is applying force to the ball to change its position.

Gravity is a force that pulls objects toward each other. Gravity keeps the moon in orbit around Earth.

A. Write the word that best completes each sentence.

direction	force	position
energy	gravity	strong

1. A _____ is a push or a pull.

2. To change the _____ of an object, you apply a force.

3. It takes _____ to apply a force.

4. A force always acts in a _____.

5. A force that pulls objects together is called _____.

6. Large objects, like Earth and the moon, have _____ gravity.

B. Write <u>True</u> if the sentence is true. Write <u>False</u> if the sentence is false.

_____ 1. A change in position always includes a change in direction.

_____ 2. Gravity pulls objects apart.

_____ 3. The amount of change in the position of the object never depends on the amount of the force applied to it.

_____ 4. Gravity cannot act on objects unless they are touching.

_____ 5. All objects have gravity.

C. Write one or more sentences to answer the question.

If all objects have gravity, why aren't you pulled toward a large building when you stand near it?

_____

_____

_____

_____

_____

_____

How Does Force Affect Motion?

A force can change the motion of an object that is already moving. In a soccer game, one player applies a force to the ball by kicking it toward the goal. A player from the other team kicks the moving ball in a different direction. The second player's kick applies a force that changes the motion of the ball. If you throw a ball straight up in the air, it does not keep going up forever. The force of gravity changes the ball's motion, causing it to fall back to the ground.

Friction is a force that resists, or works against, motion between two objects that are touching. Friction causes moving objects to slow down and stop. It applies a force that is opposite to the direction of motion. When a ball is rolled across the ground, friction between the ball and the ground works against the motion of the ball.

Friction applies a larger force to rough objects than to smooth objects. A ball rolled across a grass lawn will travel some distance. But if the same force is used to roll the ball across a smooth playground, the ball will travel farther. The smooth playground applies less friction to the ball.

Friction creates heat. You can feel the heat of friction when you rub your hands together.

Work is done whenever a force applied to an object causes the object to move in the same direction as the force. You do work when you lift a book off the floor. Gravity does work when a diver dives off a diving board. A larger force does more work than a smaller force. It takes more force to pick up a large book than a piece of paper. More work is done to lift the book. The greater the distance something moves, the more force is needed. More work is done if the book is raised to a high shelf than if it is raised to a low shelf.

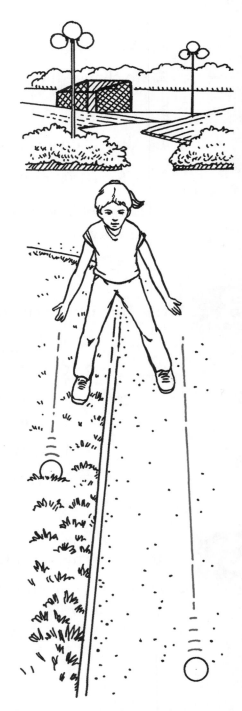

Friction resists motion between two objects. There is less friction between the smooth playground and the ball. There is more friction between the rough grass and the ball.

A. Write <u>friction</u> or <u>work</u> to answer each question.

1. What force resists, or works against, motion? _____

2. What applies a force that is opposite the direction of motion?

   _____

3. What is done when a force causes an object to move in the same direction as the force? _____

4. What applies a larger force to rough objects than to smooth objects?

   _____

B. Write the missing word in each sentence.

1. If you kick a moving soccer ball, you are applying a

   _____.

   (force, friction, gravity)

2. A ball thrown into the air falls back to the ground because of

   _____.

   (work, friction, gravity)

3. When you push a grocery cart around a supermarket, you are doing

   _____.

   (work, friction, gravity)

4. When a diver dives off a diving board, _____ does work.

   (friction, gravity, heat)

5. Rubbing two objects together creates heat because of

   _____.

   (force, friction, gravity)

C. Write one or more sentences to answer the question.

How can gravity do work? Give one example.

_____

_____

3 What Is a Lever?

If you needed to dig a hole to plant a tree, you wouldn't use your bare hands. You would probably use a shovel. A shovel is a type of simple machine. A **machine** is a tool that makes work easier. A **simple machine** is a machine that does work with only one movement. A simple machine does work by increasing a force, changing the direction of a force, or both. A simple machine does not reduce the amount of work to be done, but it does make the work easier.

A **lever** is a bar that moves around a fixed point. The fixed point is called a **fulcrum**. The object moved by a lever is called a **load**. A seesaw is one type of lever. It is balanced on a fulcrum placed at the middle of the bar. Levers with the fulcrum at the center change the direction of a force. When one end of the lever, the force, moves down, the other end, the load, moves up. When the fulcrum is closer to the load, the lever can also increase the force.

A bottle opener is a lever with the fulcrum at the opposite end from the force. The load, or bottle cap, is between them. You place the opener over the load, then lift the handle. As the handle moves up, so does the bottle cap. Because the fulcrum is at the end of the opener near the bottle cap, the lever does not change the direction of the force. But it does increase the amount of force applied by your hand to remove the bottle cap.

A hammer is a lever with the fulcrum at one end and the load at the opposite end. The force is applied between them. Like the bottle opener, this type of fulcrum does not change the direction of the force, but it does increase the force. When you use a hammer, your hand is the fulcrum. As you lower your hand to strike the nail, the hammer increases the force of your hand to drive the nail into the wood.

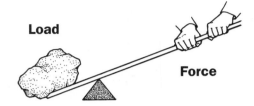

A lever with the fulcrum placed between the load to be lifted and the force doing the lifting can change the direction of a force and also increase the force.

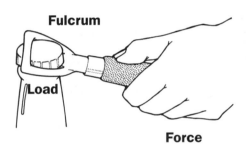

A lever with the fulcrum at the same end as the load to be moved does not change the direction of the force. It does increase the force.

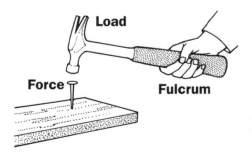

A lever with the fulcrum at the opposite end of the load to be moved does not change the direction of the force. It does increase the force.

A.

Write True if the sentence is true. Write False if the sentence is false.

_____ 1. A simple machine is a tool that makes work easier.

_____ 2. A fulcrum is a bar that moves around a fixed point.

_____ 3. A fulcrum is the fixed point on which a lever moves.

_____ 4. A load is an object moved by a lever.

_____ 5. A lever with the fulcrum at the center changes the direction of a force.

_____ 6. Levers that have the fulcrum between the load and the force change the direction of a force.

_____ 7. A lever with the fulcrum at the same end as the load increases the force.

_____ 8. A lever with the fulcrum at the end opposite the load increases the force.

B.

Draw a line to complete each sentence.

1. A playground seesaw is a lever with the fulcrum

    at the end opposite the load.

2. A bottle opener is a lever with the fulcrum

    in the center.

3. A hammer is a lever with the fulcrum

    at the same end as the load.

C.

Write one or more sentences to answer the questions.

You are sitting on one end of a playground seesaw. Your end of the seesaw is resting on the ground. Two friends climb onto the other end of the seesaw. What happens? Why? Use the words _fulcrum_ and _lever_ in your answer.

_____

_____

_____

_____

_____

129

LESSON 4

What Is a Wheel and Axle?

A **wheel and axle** is another type of simple machine. A wheel and axle is made of a disk that is attached to a post. The disk is the wheel and the post is the axle. Both the wheel and the axle turn together and in the same direction. A large turn of the wheel causes a smaller, but stronger, turn of the axle.

Anyone who has worn a pair of in-line skates or ridden a bicycle knows that wheels make work easier. Wheels that roll along the ground make work easier by reducing friction. Think about using a rope to pull a box behind you as you walk down the sidewalk. The friction of the ground rubbing against the bottom of the box makes it hard work to pull the box. If you put wheels and axles on the box, the ground rubs against the part of each wheel that touches the ground, but not the whole box. There is less friction, so the box moves much more easily.

The steering wheel on a car is a wheel and axle. A doorknob is also a wheel and axle. The handle that turns an outdoor water faucet on and off is a wheel and axle. The wheel of the faucet is the part you turn when you want to turn on the water. The wheel turns the axle, and the axle moves parts inside the faucet that allow the water to flow. Imagine trying to turn on the water by turning just the axle, with no wheel attached. It's much easier to turn the wheel. Turning the wheel a large distance turns the axle a small distance, but with a greater force. A wheel and axle increases a force, but does not change the direction of the force.

Another example of a wheel and axle is a screwdriver. A small force used to turn the handle of the screwdriver becomes a large force that can drive a screw into a piece of wood.

The wheel and axle—a simple machine—increases a force, but does not change the direction of the force. How is the bicycle in this photograph a wheel and axle?

A. Write the word or words that best complete each sentence.

axle	smaller and stronger	work
circle	wheel	
simple machine	wheel and axle	

1. A wheel and axle is a _____.

2. A _____ is like a circle-shaped disk attached to a post.

3. A _____ is shaped like a circle.

4. An _____ is shaped like a post.

5. The wheel and axle makes _____ easier.

6. Wheels and axles always turn in a _____.

7. A large turn of the wheel causes a _____ turn of the axle.

B. Write the missing word or words in each sentence.

1. Wheels _____ friction.
   (increase, reduce, do not change)

2. Wheels _____ force.
   (increase, reduce, do not change)

3. Wheels _____ the direction of a force.
   (increase, reduce, do not change)

C. Write one or more sentences to answer the question.

How is a doorknob a wheel and axle?

_____

_____

_____

_____

LESSON 5

What Is a Pulley?

A **pulley** is a rope looped around the wheel of a wheel and axle. Pulling down on the rope on one side of the pulley makes the rope on the other side of the pulley move up. Pulleys are simple machines.

Can you imagine having to climb the flagpole every time you wanted to raise or lower the flag? A pulley at the top of the flagpole makes it easier to raise the flag. The rope that is looped around the pulley is long enough to reach the ground. The flag is tied to the rope on one side of the pulley. The flag rises as you pull down on the rope on the other side. The flag moves up exactly the same distance as the length of rope you pull down. For example, if you pull down one foot of rope, the other side of the rope moves up one foot. A single pulley changes the direction of a force, but does not increase the force.

Using two or more pulleys together not only changes the direction of a force, but also increases the force. In a double pulley, a rope is looped around two pulleys. One end of the rope is attached to the object to be lifted. The free end of the rope is used to pull the object. Pulling down on the free end of the rope lifts the object. But the rope must be pulled twice the distance that the load is lifted. For example, to lift a load two feet in the air, the rope must be pulled down four feet. A double pulley makes it possible for one person to lift something that weighs more than the person weighs.

A block and tackle is a system of many pulleys used to lift very heavy objects, like airplane engines or huge steel beams. These objects may weigh thousands of pounds. Each pulley in a block and tackle helps to increase the force used to lift the load. Using many pulleys means the rope must be pulled a long distance to lift the load a short distance.

A pulley at the top of a flagpole makes it easier to raise a flag.

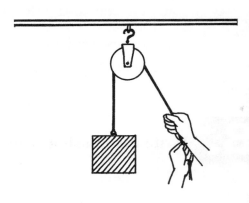

A single pulley changes the direction of a force, but does not increase the force.

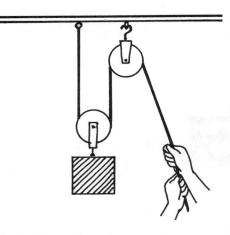

A double pulley changes the direction of the force and increases the force. A double pulley doubles the force.

132

Write <u>True</u> if the sentence is true. Write <u>False</u> if the sentence is false.

_____ 1. A pulley is a wheel with a rope looped around it.

_____ 2. Pulling down on the rope on one side of a pulley makes the rope on the other side move down.

_____ 3. Pulleys are not simple machines.

_____ 4. A single pulley is the best pulley for moving heavy objects.

_____ 5. A block and tackle does not make it easier to move heavy objects.

B. Write the missing word or words in each sentence.

1. A single pulley changes the _____ of a force.

   (amount, direction, weight)

2. A double pulley is made of _____ and one rope.

   (one pulley, two pulleys, many pulleys)

3. A block and tackle is a system of _____.

   (one pulley, many pulleys, heavy objects)

C. Draw a line to complete each sentence.

1. A single pulley   increases force.

2. A double pulley   increases force.

3. A block and tackle   does not increase force.

D. Write one or more sentences to answer the question.

How much force would be needed to lift a 200-pound object with a double pulley? Explain.

_____

_____

_____

_____

What Is an Inclined Plane?

Imagine trying to lift a heavy box from the ground so you can put it in the back of a truck. Lifting the box is hard work. What if you could push the box up a slope, or ramp, and into the truck, instead of lifting it? The ramp would make it easier to get the box from the ground into the truck.

An **inclined plane** is a slope that makes it easier to lift an object. Using an inclined plane means you have to push the object a greater distance than you would if you just lifted it. But the slope makes the work easier. An inclined plane is a simple machine that increases a force, but does not change the direction of the force. A wheelchair ramp is an inclined plane. So is a ramp in a parking garage.

A **screw** is an inclined plane that is wound around a post. Imagine using a screwdriver to twist a screw into a piece of wood. The screw changes the twisting force of the screwdriver into the downward force of the screw moving into the wood. Even though the screw has to be twisted many times, its shape makes it easier to get it into the wood. A screw changes the direction of a force and increases the force. Screw-cap bottles and jars use screws to open and close their lids. Nuts and bolts are also screws.

A **wedge** is two inclined planes placed back to back. A wedge has a sharp edge and can cut or pry things apart. An ax is a wedge. Someone using an ax to split wood applies a force to push the sharp end of the wedge into the wood. As the wedge moves into the wood, it pushes the wood apart. A wedge changes the downward force of the ax to a sideways force. A wedge changes the direction of a force and increases the force. A pair of scissors is made of two moveable wedges. A knife is also a wedge.

The gradual slope of an inclined plane makes it easier to lift something heavy.

A screw is an inclined plane wound around a post.

A wedge is two inclined planes fastened together, as in the head of an ax.

A. Write an inclined plane, a screw, or a wedge to complete each sentence.

1. A slope that makes it easier to lift objects is _____.

2. The direction of a force is not changed by _____.

3. An inclined plane wrapped around a post is _____.

4. A turning force is changed into a downward force by

    _____.

5. Two inclined planes fastened together make _____.

6. You can use _____ to cut.

B. Write the missing word or words in each sentence.

1. An example of a screw is a _____.
   (parking garage ramp, jar lid, knife)

2. An example of a wedge is a _____.
   (parking garage ramp, jar lid, knife)

3. An example of an inclined plane is a _____.
   (parking garage ramp, jar lid, knife)

C. Write one or more sentences to answer the question.

You have several tiny wedges in your body. What are they?

_____

_____

_____

_____

_____

_____

CHAPTER 8

Test Friction

You need:

- **paper**
- **pencil**
- **ruler**
- **book**
- **wood block**
- **construction paper**
- **tape**
- **sandpaper**
- **aluminum foil**

Test Friction	
Surface	Height
Book	
Construction Paper	
Sandpaper	

In this activity you will test how friction affects a sliding object.

Follow these steps:

1. Make a chart with five spaces to record notes.

2. Hold the ruler upright next to the book. Place the wood block on the book next to the ruler.

3. Slowly raise the end of the book next to the ruler. Stop when the wood block moves.

4. Note the mark on the ruler nearest the bottom edge of the book. Write it on your chart.

5. Tape construction paper over the top of the book and repeat Steps 2 through 4.

6. Repeat Steps 2 through 4 three more times, after covering the book with sandpaper, aluminum foil, and something that you choose.

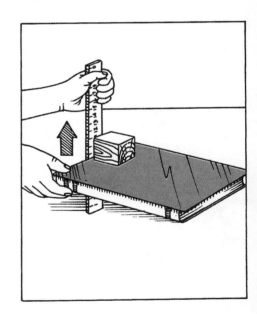

Write answers to these questions.

1. Which surface created the most friction with the wood block?

2. Which surface created the least friction with the wood block? How could you make even less friction between the wood block and the book?

Darken the circle next to the correct answer.

1. A push or pull that changes the position of an object is
   Ⓐ friction.
   Ⓑ gravity.
   Ⓒ a force.
   Ⓓ a simple machine.

2. The force that pulls two objects toward each other is
   Ⓐ friction.
   Ⓑ gravity.
   Ⓒ light energy.
   Ⓓ heat.

3. The force that resists motion between two objects that are touching is
   Ⓐ friction.
   Ⓑ gravity.
   Ⓒ light energy.
   Ⓓ heat.

4. Work is done when a force moves an object
   Ⓐ in the same direction as the force.
   Ⓑ in the opposite direction from the force.
   Ⓒ straight up only.
   Ⓓ more than the length of the object.

5. A machine that does work with only one movement is a
   Ⓐ one-step machine.
   Ⓑ simple machine.
   Ⓒ one-moving-part tool.
   Ⓓ mechanical tool.

6. What is a bar that moves around a fixed point called?
   Ⓐ a wheel and axle
   Ⓑ an inclined plane
   Ⓒ a lever
   Ⓓ a pulley

7. A doorknob is an example of what kind of simple machine?
   Ⓐ a wheel and axle
   Ⓑ an inclined plane
   Ⓒ a lever
   Ⓓ a pulley

8. What kind of simple machine is a wheel with a rope looped around it?
   Ⓐ a wheel and axle
   Ⓑ an inclined plane
   Ⓒ a lever
   Ⓓ a pulley

9. A wheelchair ramp is an example of what kind of simple machine?
   Ⓐ a wheel and axle
   Ⓑ an inclined plane
   Ⓒ a lever
   Ⓓ a pulley

10. What is an inclined plane that is wrapped around a post called?
    Ⓐ an inclined post
    Ⓑ a wedge
    Ⓒ a screwdriver
    Ⓓ a screw

Careers

Recording Engineer

When you watch a movie or listen to a song on the radio, a recording engineer has worked hard to make the sounds, music, or sound effects you hear.

Recording engineers run the machines that record sounds. Recording engineers use microphones and tape recorders to do this. They also use headphones to listen to their recordings. If a recording does not sound right, recording engineers fix it.

Auto Mechanic

An auto mechanic services and repairs cars. Some auto mechanics work only on buses or trucks. If a car breaks down, then an auto mechanic must figure out what is wrong and fix it. Auto mechanics also do work that keeps a car from breaking down. They check parts for wear. Auto mechanics repair, rebuild, or replace parts on a car.

Mechanical Engineer

Before astronauts could fly to the moon, mechanical engineers had to think of a way to make a rocket engine that could get them there.

A mechanical engineer designs, runs, and tests all kinds of machines. Mechanical engineers work on computers, airplanes, and printing presses. In fact, almost any kind of machine you can think of was invented or worked on by mechanical engineers.

Glossary

A **adapt**, page 34.
Living things adapt when they adjust to life under different conditions.

adaptation, page 34.
An adaptation is a characteristic of an animal that helps it survive.

air mass, page 96.
An air mass is a huge body of air that forms above a large area of land or water.

air pressure, page 94.
Air pressure is caused by the weight of the air in the atmosphere.

altitude, page 90.
Altitude is the distance above sea level.

amphibians, page 28.
Amphibians are animals that live part of their lives in water and part on land.

anemometer, page 96.
An anemometer measures wind speed.

aquatic biomes, page 68.
Aquatic biomes are areas where plants and animals live in water.

arctic air mass, page 96.
An arctic air mass is a very cold air mass.

arteries, page 44.
Arteries are blood vessels that carry oxygen-rich blood from the heart to the rest of the body.

atmosphere, page 82.
The atmosphere is the air that surrounds Earth.

B **barometers**, page 94.
Barometers measure air pressure.

biome, page 58.
A biome is a large place with a certain climate and plants and animals adapted to that climate.

bladder, page 50.
The bladder stores waste liquid from the kidneys until it can leave the body.

blood, page 42.
Blood is a liquid that travels throughout the body, bringing oxygen to the cells and taking carbon dioxide away.

blood vessels, page 44.
Blood vessels—arteries, veins, and capillaries—are the tubes through which blood travels.

bones, page 40.
Bones are hard tissue that makes up your skeleton.

bony fish, page 26.
Bony fish have skeletons made mostly of bone.

burrows, page 64.
Burrows are underground homes for some small grassland animals, such as gophers.

C **canopy**, page 66.
The canopy is the top part, or roof, of the rain forest.

capillaries, page 44.
Capillaries are tiny blood vessels in the human body where the exchange of oxygen and carbon dioxide happens.

carbon dioxide, pages 42 and 82.
Carbon dioxide is a gas in the air. Plants use it to make food. Animals breathe it out as a waste.

cartilage, page 26.
Cartilage is a tough tissue, like the hard tissue in your outer ear.

circulatory system, page 44.
Your circulatory system has three parts—the blood, the heart, and the blood vessels.

climate, page 58.
Climate is formed by the temperature and rainfall patterns of an area.

coal, page 80.
Coal is a fossil fuel made from dead plants that were buried before they decomposed completely.

cold front, page 98.
A cold front forms when a cold air mass pushes under a warm air mass, forcing the warm air up.

compost, page 76.
Compost is natural waste that has decayed into soil filled with nutrients.

condensation, page 92.
Condensation is the process in which a gas changes into a liquid.

conduction, page 110.
Conduction is the flow of heat through the movement of molecules in a solid object or from one object to an object it is touching.

conifers, page 12.
Conifers are trees and shrubs that hold their seeds in cones. Pine trees and fir trees are both conifers.

continental air mass, page 96.
A continental air mass has low humidity.

contracts, page 96.
When something contracts, its molecules move closer together.

convection, page 110.
Convection is the circular motion of heat through liquids or gases.

D **deciduous**, page 66.
Deciduous trees lose their leaves in autumn and grow new ones every spring. Deciduous forests are forests that have many deciduous trees.

decompose, page 80.
When materials decompose, they break down into simpler materials.

deserts, page 62.
Deserts are the driest biomes, receiving less than ten inches of rain in a year.

diaphragm, page 46.
The diaphragm is a smooth muscle stretched across the bottom of your lungs. When it contracts, it gets flatter and pulls the lungs down to help you breathe.

digestive system, page 48.
Your digestive system turns the food you eat into fuel that runs your body.

dinosaurs, page 32.
Dinosaurs were reptiles that appeared about 230 million years ago. They ruled Earth for more than 140 million years.

domesticated plants, page 18.
Domesticated plants have been kept separate from their wild ancestors and grown under controlled conditions.

E **electrical energy**, page 112.
Electrical energy is a form of energy produced by batteries and power plants.

electromagnetic radiation, page 118.
Electromagnetic radiation is all the kinds of energy given off by the sun. The sun is not the only source.

electromagnetic spectrum, page 118.
The electromagnetic spectrum is formed by all the different kinds of electromagnetic radiation.

erosion, page 76.
Erosion happens when rain and wind carry away the richest top layers of soil.

esophagus, page 48.
The esophagus is the tube leading from your mouth to your stomach.

evaporation, page 92.
Evaporation is the process in which a liquid changes into a gas.

evergreens, page 60.
Evergreens are plants that stay green all year.

excretory system, page 50.
The excretory system carries wastes out of the body.

exosphere, page 90.
The exosphere is the topmost layer that is found in Earth's atmosphere.

expands, page 94.
When something expands, it spreads out.

extinct, page 8.
Extinct means that a certain kind of living thing is no longer alive.

F **ferns**, page 12.
Ferns are leafy, green plants that grow well in shady, damp places.

fertilizer, page 76.
Fertilizer is a special nutrient that is added to soil to make it richer for plants.

flowering plants, page 14.
Flowering plants produce seeds in flowers.

force, page 124.
A force is a push or a pull that changes the position of an object.

forecast, page 98.
To forecast is to tell what may happen with the weather.

forests, page 66.
Forests are biomes that have many trees growing close together.

fossil fuels, page 80.
Fossil fuels, such as petroleum, natural gas, and coal, formed under the ground from the remains of plants and animals that lived millions of years ago.

fossils, page 8.
Fossils are traces of early life that have been preserved in rocks.

friction, page 126.
Friction is a force that resists, or works against, motion between two objects that are touching.

front, page 98.
A front is the zone formed where two air masses with different properties meet.

fulcrum, page 128.
A fulcrum is the fixed point around which a lever moves.

G gamma rays, page 118.
Gamma rays are the shortest waves of energy in the electromagnetic spectrum. They travel through almost any material.

generator, page 114.
A generator is a machine that changes mechanical energy to electrical energy.

gills, page 68.
Gills are special body parts that animals, like fish, use to take in oxygen from the water around them.

grasslands, page 64.
Grasslands are dry biomes that get more rain than deserts, but not enough steady rain for a large number of trees to grow.

gravity, page 82.
Gravity is a force that pulls objects toward each other. Earth's gravity pulls on any object.

groundwater, page 92.
Groundwater is formed by precipitation that sinks deep within Earth.

H hard-bodied, page 24.
Hard-bodied animals are animals with bones or shells supporting their bodies.

heart, page 44.
The heart is a special muscle that pumps blood throughout the body.

heat, page 108.
Heat is energy that moves from a warmer object to a cooler object.

humidity, page 92.
Humidity is the amount of water vapor in the air.

hurricane, page 100.
A hurricane is a dangerous storm that forms over the ocean.

hybrid plants, page 18.
Hybrid plants result when people combine two different plant species.

I inclined plane, page 134.
An inclined plane is a simple machine. It is a slope that makes it easier to lift objects.

infrared radiation, page 118.
Infrared radiation is another name for heat energy. It is found just above radio waves in the electromagnetic spectrum.

insects, page 28.
Insects are tiny invertebrates with six legs.

intestines, page 48.
The walls of the small intestine soak up tiny pieces of food. The large intestine draws water out of the remaining food.

invertebrates, page 26.
Invertebrates are animals without backbones.

involuntary muscles, page 40.
Involuntary muscles are the muscles that move even when you are sleeping.

J jawed fish, page 26.
Jawed fish can bite and hold food in their mouths.

jawless fish, page 26.
Jawless fish have a sucker mouth instead of jaws. Examples include lampreys.

joints, page 40.
The bones in your skeleton are connected at joints.

K kidneys, page 50.
The kidneys remove waste from your blood.

kinetic energy, page 114.
Kinetic energy is the mechanical energy in moving objects.

L lever, page 128.
A lever is a bar that moves around a fixed point.

light energy, page 112.
Light energy is a form of energy that can travel through empty space and through clear objects.

load, page 128.
The load is the object moved by a lever.

lungs, page 46.
The lungs are where oxygen is brought into the body and carbon dioxide is removed.

M machine, page 128.
A machine is a tool that makes work easier.

mammals, page 34.
Mammals are vertebrates with hair on their bodies. They feed milk to their young.

marine biomes, page 68.
Marine biomes, or saltwater biomes, include all the oceans of the world.

maritime air mass, page 96.
A maritime air mass has high humidity.

mechanical energy, page 112.
Mechanical energy is the energy of moving objects.

mesosphere, page 90.
The mesosphere is the layer of air above the stratosphere and below the thermosphere.

meteorologists, page 94.
Meteorologists are people who study weather.

microwaves, page 118.
Microwaves are radio waves used in radar and in some ovens to cook food.

minerals, page 78.
Minerals are metals and shiny stones that are found under the ground.

mining, page 76.
Mining is taking natural resources like coal and metals from the ground.

molecules, pages 92 and 108.
Molecules are the smallest particles of a substance, such as water.

muscles, page 40.
Muscles allow you to move your bones.

N natural gas, page 80.
Natural gas is a fossil fuel that forms underground from petroleum if temperatures are high enough.

natural resources, page 74.
Natural resources are living and nonliving things found on Earth that help people meet their needs.

nectar, page 14.
Nectar is food for insects made by flowering plants.

nitrogen, page 82.
Nitrogen is the most plentiful gas in air.

nonrenewable resources, page 74.
Nonrenewable resources are such things as oil and coal that are present on Earth in limited amounts.

O ore, page 78.
Ore is rock that contains a large amount of a certain mineral such as iron.

oxygen, page 82.
Oxygen is one of the gases that make up air. Animals need it to live. Plants give it off as waste.

ozone, page 90.
The ozone layer in Earth's stratosphere protects us from the sun's harmful rays.

P petroleum, page 80.
Petroleum, or crude oil, is a sticky, liquid fossil fuel.

phloem, page 12.
Phloem tissues carry food made by plants during photosynthesis.

photosynthesis, page 8.
Photosynthesis is the process in which plants use sunlight to make food.

plankton, page 68.
Plankton are tiny plants and animals that float at the surface of the ocean.

plasma, page 42.
Plasma is a yellow liquid made mostly of water. It acts as a stream in which the red and white blood cells and platelets float.

platelets, page 42.
Platelets are the smallest of the blood cells. They allow your blood to clot.

polar air mass, page 96.
A polar air mass is a cold air mass.

pollen, page 14.
Pollen is a yellow dust that flowering plants make to help them reproduce.

pollination, page 14.
Pollination is the process in which flowering plants use pollen to make seeds.

pollute, page 76.
People pollute the soil, air, and water by placing harmful materials in them.

potential energy, page 114.
Potential energy is the mechanical energy that is stored in nonmoving objects that can move.

precipitation, page 60.
Precipitation includes rain and snow.

pulley, page 132.
A pulley is a simple machine. It is a rope looped around a wheel.

R **radar**, page 100.
From Earth, weather radar tracks the movement and speed of storms.

radiation, page 110.
Radiation is the movement of heat energy through empty space, as from the sun to Earth.

radio waves, page 118.
Radio waves are the longest waves in the electromagnetic spectrum. They are used to broadcast radio and television programs.

rain forests, page 66.
Rain forests are forest biomes that receive from 80 to 200 or more inches of rain a year.

red blood cells, page 42.
Red blood cells carry oxygen from the air you breathe to all the parts of your body. They carry carbon dioxide, or waste gas, that body cells do not need to the lungs.

renewable resources, page 74.
Renewable resources are such things as plants and animals that can never be used up if they are used properly.

reproduce, page 14.
When living things reproduce, they make new living things of the same species.

reptiles, page 30.
Reptiles are vertebrates with dry, scaly skin.

respiratory system, page 46.
The respiratory system includes the trachea, lungs, and diaphragm.

runoff, page 92.
Runoff is precipitation that flows on Earth's surface.

S **saliva**, page 48.
Saliva is a liquid made in your mouth.

saltwater, pages 68 and 84.
Saltwater, like the water in the oceans, contains salt.

satellites, page 100.
From above Earth's atmosphere, weather satellites collect information about the atmosphere and send it back to Earth.

savanna, page 58.
A savanna is a grassland in Africa.

screw, page 134.
A screw is a simple machine made up of an inclined plane wound around a post.

sea level, page 94.
Sea level is where the air meets the ocean.

simple machine, page 128.
A simple machine is a machine that does work with only one movement.

soft-bodied, page 24.
Soft-bodied animals are animals without bones or shells for body support.

soil, page 76.
Soil is the top layer of Earth's surface. It is made of tiny pieces of rocks mixed with natural waste, such as dead leaves.

solar energy, page 92.
Solar energy is heat energy from the sun.

solar heaters, page 116.
Solar heaters capture the sun's energy.

sound energy, page 112.
Sound energy is a form of energy that can travel through air, water, metal, and other materials.

species, page 14.
A species is a group of living things of one kind.

stationary front, page 98.
A stationary front forms when a warm air mass and a cold air mass meet and neither air mass moves.

stomach, page 48.
The stomach stores food and mixes it with chemicals that break the food down.

stratosphere, page 90.
The stratosphere is the layer of air above the troposphere and below the mesosphere.

T **taiga**, page 60.
The taiga is one of the coldest biomes. It is an evergreen forest with long winters.

temperature, page 108.
Temperature is a measure of how hot or cold something is.

tendons, page 40.
Tendons are strong, elastic tissues that attach muscles to bones.

thermometers, page 94.
Thermometers measure temperature.

thermosphere, page 90.
The thermosphere is the layer of air above the mesosphere and below the exosphere.

tornado, page 100.
A tornado is a dangerous storm that forms over land.

trachea, page 46.
The trachea is the main air tube, leading from your nose and mouth to your lungs.

tropical air mass, page 96.
A tropical air mass is a warm air mass.

tropics, page 66.
The tropics are parts of the world where temperatures are warm all year.

troposphere, page 90.
The troposphere is the layer of air that is closest to Earth's surface.

tundra, page 60.
The tundra is one of the coldest biomes. For most of the year, the tundra is a frozen grassland.

turbine, page 114.
A turbine is a kind of giant fan used in power plants to run a generator.

U ultraviolet light, page 118.
Ultraviolet light is just above visible light in the electromagnetic spectrum. It causes sunburn.

V vascular plants, page 12.
Vascular plants are plants that have special tissues called xylem and phloem.

veins, page 44.
Veins are blood vessels that carry blood filled with carbon dioxide to the heart.

vertebrates, page 26.
Vertebrates are animals with backbones.

visible light, page 118.
Visible light is the only part of the electromagnetic spectrum that human eyes can see. Visible light waves are slightly shorter than infrared waves.

voluntary muscles, page 40.
Voluntary muscles are the muscles that move your skeleton. You can move them when you want to.

W warm front, page 98.
A warm front forms when a warm air mass pushes up and over a cold air mass.

water cycle, page 92.
The water cycle is the way water changes form and moves in Earth's atmosphere and on land.

water vapor, page 92.
Water vapor is the gas that liquid water changes into when it gains enough heat energy.

weather stations, page 100.
Weather stations are places where meteorologists set up weather equipment.

weather vane, page 96.
A weather vane measures wind direction.

wedge, page 134.
A wedge is a simple machine made up of two inclined planes placed back to back.

wheel and axle, page 130.
A wheel and axle is a simple machine made up of a disk attached to a post.

white blood cells, page 42.
White blood cells act as the body's soldiers against disease. They move to where germs are and work to destroy them.

wind, page 96.
Wind is the movement of air.

windbreaks, page 76.
Windbreaks are rows of trees that help block erosion of soil by the wind.

work, page 126.
Work is done whenever a force applied to an object causes the object to move in the same direction as the force.

X X-rays, page 118.
X-rays are the second shortest waves of energy in the electromagnetic spectrum. They pass through skin and muscle, but are absorbed by bone.

xylem, page 12.
Xylem tissues carry water and nutrients throughout the plant.